A Halloween Homicide

David W Robinson

A Halloween Homicide: 978-1-908910-31-8

Printed for Crooked Cat Publishing by Createspace

First Black Line Edition, Crooked Cat Publishing Ltd. 2012

Discover us online:
www.crookedcatpublishing.com

Join us on facebook:
www.facebook.com/crookedcatpublishing

The Author

A Yorkshireman by birth, David Robinson is a retired hypnotherapist and former adult education teacher, now living on the outskirts of Manchester with his wife and crazy Jack Russell called Joe (because he looks like a Joe).

A freelance writer for almost 30 years, he is extensively published, mainly on the web and in small press magazines. His first two novels were published in 2002 and are no longer available. His third novel, The Haunting at Melmerby Manor was published by Virtual Tales (USA) in 2007. He writes in a number of genres, including crime, sci-fi, horror and humour, and all his work has an element of mystery. His alter-ego, Flatcap, looks at the modern world from a cynical, 3rd age perspective, employing various levels of humour from subtle to sledgehammer.

A devout follower of Manchester United, when he is not writing, he enjoys photography, cryptic crosswords, and putting together slideshow trailers and podcast readings from his works.

A Halloween Homicide is the third in the series of Sanford 3rd Age Mystery novels. The Filey Connection and The I-Spy Murders are also available at Amazon and from other good online retailers.

David's online blog is at: **http://www.dwrob.com**

By the same author

The STAC Mystery series:

Other work:

A Halloween Homicide

Chapter One

Edgar Prudhoe, MP, cut the connection, closed his clamshell mobile and dropped it into his shirt pocket. "Done deal," he said to his wife.

Deidre returned a sour glance over her grapefruit half. "Anyone would think you've just bought the place."

The broad grin on Edgar's tanned face slackened and faded. There were times when, with the best will in the world, he could not remember why he married Deidre. When he tried to recall those far off days of the mid to late 1980s, he could remember the music, the parties, the drink and the drugs, and the first time they spent the night together had remained firmly entrenched in his memory; a field in Glastonbury, Van Morrison, Elvis Costello, The Mighty Lemondrops, *Carhenge* built by the Mutoid Waste Company, trouble with travellers, the inevitable field of mud in the rain, and so many drugs on open sale. Sex under canvas and Deidre smacked out of her head most of the time. He was 21 years old, life was dynamite on a short fuse and exploded in a hedonistic joy of life.

Two years later, they were married with a daughter on the way, and he couldn't remember why he had decided to marry her. And it must have been he who decided. Deidre didn't make decisions. Deidre *couldn't* make decisions. If someone gave her an order (him for instance) she would either get on with it or return a tirade of verbal abuse as a refusal, but that depended on her mood and not an ability to actually make decisions.

So what had happened in those intervening two years to

change him from Mr wild, free and willing, to Mr average, marrying Mrs average in an average church in an average Lincolnshire town and then settling down in the average detached pad in the average suburb?

Whatever it was, he often found himself wishing he could travel back in time, intercept his younger self on the way to the church and say, "Run for it. Get the hell out of here, now."

Popping his blood pressure pill onto his tongue, washing it down with a mouthful of freshly squeezed orange juice, he realised how selfish and unfair that thought was. Deidre had not been a bad wife. To his knowledge, she had never been unfaithful, and when they put on those lavish dinner parties, she was always immaculately turned out, the perfect hostess. She never complained about the time he had to spend in London and she never hassled him to take her along. When constituency matters called him to his local office on Saturday morning, cancelling any plans they had made for the weekend, she didn't protest, and when election time came round, she was out with him every day, canvassing from dawn to dusk and beyond. Twice now, she had stood in the hall listening to his acceptance speech, applauding, supportive, just as the dutiful wife should.

But privately, she was a mess. She didn't bother dressing most days, crawling out of bed in the middle of the day, lounging around in pyjamas and a dressing gown, smoking cigarette after cigarette, knocking back the vodka like it was lemonade. Coming up to her 48th birthday, her strawberry blonde hair was now straw, straggling about her thin face like seaweed clogging the propeller shaft of a cabin cruiser. Her small, once proud breasts sagged when they had no support and those legs, which had so attracted him back in the 80s, now reminded him of pipe cleaners; thin and wrinkled.

By contrast, he had maintained much of his youthful looks. Not by good luck, but by sheer hard work. Three sessions a week in the gym (Westminster when the House was sitting, home when it wasn't) followed by a strenuous swim, careful dieting, only moderate drinking and no smoking. He was a man of force, someone to be reckoned with; but he was married to a rambling, sexless weed.

Not that the latter troubled him unduly. There were natural compensations for the successful politician: other women upon whose attentions he could call when he felt the need. Nothing serious, certainly nothing long-term, but mutually satisfying adventures filling lazy afternoons in his Kensington flat. And if he felt the slightest hint of guilt, it was easy to rationalise. Those hours of fun helped keep him sane and allowed him to remain married to Deidre.

Arguments were infrequent, but that was largely because Deidre rarely spoke to him or anyone else other than in her semi-official capacity as the Honourable Member's wife. And when they did exchange words, it was usually her delivering the more forceful invective.

Lifeless. That's what the marriage was. Lifeless. And not his fault. Deidre's. The woman simply had no get up and go. Hadn't he just arranged a special treat for their daughter's 21st birthday? Hannah, he knew, would be over the moon with the deal. Expensive hotel, ghost hunt and all that Halloween palaver. But Deidre... her apathy made him feel like...

"You make it sound as if I've just ordered a pizza."

Deidre swallowed a mouthful of orange juice. Edgar wondered how much vodka was in the glass.

"You've arranged a weekend at a hotel for her 21st birthday. I could have done that."

"No," Edgar disagreed. "You wouldn't be able to decide which hotel."

Deidre did not rise to the jibe. With a huff, Edgar picked up *The Telegraph* and read the gloomy headlines again. After years in opposition, now forming part of the coalition government, the party's fortunes were wavering. Only to be expected, he thought. The government of the day was always the least popular of political colours.

He gazed across the vast expanse of lawn to where his daughter and her boyfriend lay, baring obscene amounts of flesh to the warm September sunshine. Hannah was very much the image of her mother in those far off days of Glastonbury. Rakishly thin yet curvaceous and attractive, with a naughty gleam in her hazel eyes.

His stare shifted and focussed on the lean, muscular body laid alongside Hannah. Edgar's lip curled. Callum bloody McGuire. Twenty-two years old, fitter than any dog belonging to any butcher, a bloody chancer who had set his sights on Hannah when they met at university and he realised who her prominent father was. A fortune hunter or Edgar had never seen one. Oh, he was all right on the surface; very much 'yes, sir, I quite agree, sir, you have a point there, sir'. Claimed to have supported the party for years and couldn't help himself agreeing with every word Edgar said; even those words decrying the values of modern students.

Hannah was completely taken in by him, but Callum McGuire would have to get out of bed early to fool Edgar Prudhoe. And he'd have to get out of bed even earlier before he could get his grubby Scottish hands on the Prudhoe money.

***

Cal yawned, shifted his sunglasses onto his forehead and glanced to his left at Hannah's closed eyes. Lowering the shades again, he turned his head to look in the opposite direction, towards the patio where Edgar and Deidre were having a midday breakfast. Deidre looked drunk – nothing new there – and Edgar was glowering in his direction. Nothing new there, either.

Cal turned his head once more to face Hannah. "Your dad doesn't like me, Hann."

She stirred, her ruby lips forming a pout. Rolling onto her side, she stared into Cal's deep blue eyes and smiled. "Dads are like that, Cal. If I came home with the crown prince of wherever hanging on my arm, he still wouldn't be good enough for my old man."

"It goes deeper than that," Cal replied, his Edinburgh burr contrasting sharply with her soft, Lincolnshire accent. "He really hates me."

She laughed, a silly, girlish giggle. "You're paranoid. Look at the time you said old Dickerson had a downer on you because he only gave you an A instead of an A-plus in media studies."

"I was right," Cal protested. "That video was worth an A-plus. He was just irritated because it was better than anything he could do. Anyway, I wasn't talking about Dickerson. I was talking about your dad. He's glaring at me now. I can feel his eyes burning into the back of my head."

Hann raised herself up onto one elbow and looked across at her father. She gave him a twee smile and he smiled back indulgently. "He thinks you're a gold digger," she said. "He thinks all my boyfriends are gold diggers."

"All your boyfriends?" Cal teased. "How many more are there besides me?"

Hann lay back on her tummy, her head resting in folded arms, and laughed again. "That's for me to know." She yawned. "It's one of the worries of having a father who's filthy rich, I s'ppose. One day all this will be mine." She gestured around the vast garden with her eyes. "Along with the untold zillions he has tucked away in the bank."

"But not until daddy pops his clogs."

"Pops his clogs? Where on earth did you hear that?"

"Had to do a bit of research on idioms during my final year," Cal said, "and that was one of the expressions the tutor gave me. Comes from the North, where working people used to wear clogs. To pop means to pawn them, and it means the widow would pawn the husband's boots when he died. Pop his clogs. It came to mean someone's death."

"Quaint," Hann agreed. "Well, yes, I suppose when Daddy

pops his clogs I'll be a wealthy socialite. Until then, he keeps an eye on my boyfriends." She grinned again. "If you want your share of Daddy's money, you'd better marry me quick."

Cal returned her grin. "All right. Will you marry me?"

"No. I want to finish university, then go round the world and have an adventure before I settle down." She pulled her tongue out at him. "So you'll just have to wait to get your hands on my money."

Hann turned her face away from him to sleep. Cal did likewise, but found himself staring into Edgar's angry eyes again, so he turned once more and looked at the back of Hann's head instead, inhaling the tantalising essence of her fair hair and imagining that hair spread across the pillows beneath him.

"I wish you would pop your clogs you miserable old sod."

***

One hour later and a hundred miles to the north, Joe Murray looked out through windows of the top room at the Miner's Arms and tried to ignore the protests coming at him from the monthly meeting of the Sanford Third Age Club.

After a sweltering summer, the whole of Great Britain yearned for the cool of autumn, but there was no sign of an end to the heat wave yet, and the country baked in early September temperatures way above the norm. Outside, a heat haze wafted up from the dust dry road, bikers roared past devoid of leathers, couples and families strolled along in shirt sleeves and shorts, and the tables of the beer garden behind the pub were packed with Sunday lunchtime drinkers.

Joe would give his right arm to be with them, enjoying a cool beer in the heat of the day, or sat in his back yard at home, reading and enjoying a beer of his own, straight from the chiller. Anything other than dealing with the rabble of third agers looking for trouble.

He, Sheila Riley and Brenda Jump, as the management trio

8

of the club, were seated on the podium, facing about 150 of STAC's 300-strong membership, and Joe had never seen them in such a belligerent mood. Ever since the meeting began on the stroke of noon, they had argued with him, argued with each other, argued with Mick Chadwick, the landlord, and then argued with themselves again. It was as if the months of unrelenting heat had taken its toll on their tolerance, and they had decided that now was the time to vent the ill-feeling.

They were a motley assortment. Some were widowed, some were divorced, others were still locked in happy or otherwise marriages. Some were still working, others had given it up through retirement, failing health, or simple unemployment. They represented a range of working types; professional, skilled, unskilled, clerical, practical, managerial. But the one thing they had in common was their age: everyone was over fifty. Many were at that time of life when every day the grim reaper did not come to call was a bonus, most had come to the conclusion that if life was a game of two halves, they were well into the second half. All had decided that now was the time to start enjoying life, and without exception they would argue black was white to secure whatever pleasure they could.

In the centre of the crowd, Alec Staines exchanged harsh words with Cyril Peck, Alec jabbing a threatening finger at the air to ram home his point, while Cyril's toothless mouth curled into a contemptuous, 'you-wouldn't-dare' scowl. Les Tanner debated with his lady friend, Sylvia Goodson, shaking his head at something she said, and towards the rear of the room, George Robson gritted his teeth at something Mavis Barker was saying.

Third agers, Joe thought. Like born again children. Who'd have 'em?

Inhaling deeply, he rapped his pen on the table. "Let's have a bitta hush, people," he shouted above the mutinous hubbub. "Come on, calm it down and let me explain."

Seated at a table near the front, his regimental tie snuggled neatly under his Adam's apple, pristine white shirt gleaming in the early afternoon sunshine, Captain Les Tanner laid a gimlet eye on the chairman. "There's nothing to explain, Murray, only your usual level of inefficiency."

Stung into retaliation, Joe snapped, "That's smart coming from a council pen pusher."

Someone at the rear of the room said, "Hear, hear," and a further chorus of rhubarb anger rumbled across the meeting.

Joe rapped on the table again. "Come on, folks. Calm it down. We're gonna be here all day at this rate, and it won't change nothing."

It was like trying to bring silence to a crowd at a football match.

Alongside him, Brenda got to her feet and raised her voice. "Shut… up!"

Silence fell; a silence broken only by the rattle of bottles beneath the bar where landlord Mick Chadwick was restocking the chiller.

"For all your whinging," Brenda went on, "Joe works his socks off for this club and he does the best he can. You asked him for a spooky weekend over Halloween and he's arranged it."

"We appreciate that, Brenda," Sylvia Goodson said in a voice calculated to pour oil on the troubled waters, "but we wanted to be together; all of us."

"Then you should have said something earlier," Joe argued, taking the stand from Brenda again. On his other side, Sheila Riley wrote furiously, keeping the minutes of the meeting. "You keeping up with this?" he asked and she nodded. "If I'm speaking too fast, say something," he told her, and turned to address his audience again. "At July's meeting you asked for a Christmas weekend away, which I've arranged, and the details will be circulated once we get the leaflets from the Regency Hotel. Christmas is still sixteen weeks away. Then last month, you asked for a Halloween weekend. Halloween is less than nine weeks, and you think I can just drop onto a hotel and have them supply seventy to a hundred rooms, AND include spooky entertainment AND a ghost hunt? I'm a wizard in the kitchen, not the travel agency."

"If you're a wizard does that make Sheila and Brenda witches?" George Robson called out. "Only the last steak and kidney pie I had at your place…"

The rest of George's remarks were drowned out in another sea of recrimination.

Joe rattled for attention again and this time, Sheila stood up with the relevant documentation in her hand.

"Here's what we managed to arrange," she said when order was once again restored. "We managed to get ten of you into rooms at The Feathers, Pocklington. It's reputed to be haunted and there will be some form of entertainment on Halloween. Forty more rooms have been secured at The Palmer Hotel, near Elvington. The place has an old inn and stable house at the rear which is also reported to be haunted, and they're putting on a midnight ghost hunt. The rest of you will stay at The Steeplechase Hotel, in York, and there will be an organised ghost walk during the evening of the 31st. Given the short notice, it was the best we could do."

Joe stood again. "We've allocated the accommodation by lot, making sure that when a name came out of the hat, that name's friends and-or spouse was lodged in the same accommodation."

"You could have had Alec for the weekend, Brenda," Julia Staines called out.

"Don't tempt her," Joe suggested. "Now, if you're not happy with the situation and you want to withdraw, let us know. We have to pay the bills by the week after next, and I don't want to be paying for rooms that will not be taken."

"How come you couldn't book us all into the one place?" Les Tanner demanded, "The Palmer, for instance?"

"Because the place only has fifty rooms," Sheila reported. The Steeplechase didn't have sufficient vacancies and when we inquired of The Feathers, the five rooms we booked there were the only ones remaining."

"Halloween," Joe said. "It wasn't like this when we were kids, but we seem to have imported the party spirit from the States and we're stuck with it. Everywhere is full."

"All I can say is, I hope the Christmas do is arranged better than this," Tanner grumbled.

Joe's lip curled. "And all I can say is, I wish you bods at the town hall could arrange the public services as well as we do these outings."

His remark prompted another round of accusation and counter accusation, threat and counter threat before Sheila and Brenda restored order.

After a brief and whispered conversation between the two women, Brenda stood again.

"It's going to be a logistical nightmare for the coaches, I'm afraid. They'll drop us all in York at about ten in the morning, so we can do a little shopping. We'll be collected at four in the afternoon so we can be taken to our respective hotels. You're going to have to make sure you're on the correct bus."

"And how will we know which bus we're on?" Tanner demanded.

"We'll be sorting everything out this week," Joe told him. "The emails will go out Friday, and they'll have all your details on them."

From the back of the room, Mavis Barker said something, but Joe could not hear it for landlord Mick dropping several bottles from his stack.

With a frown at the landlord, Joe said, "Say again, Mavis."

"I said," she repeated a little louder this time, "I hope you get it right. I don't want to end up spending the night with George for company."

Joe buried his head in his hands as the room collapsed into disorder again.

Chapter Two

Carrying his briefcase, Edgar turned up his collar for the dash from the Bentley into The Palmer Hotel Reception. Deidre, sheltering beneath a dark blue umbrella, followed at a more leisurely pace, taking a final drag on her cigarette before crushing it on the wall-mounted stubber by the doors.

"Come on, woman," Edgar urged. "I'd like to get checked in and grab some lunch."

Deidre turned back. "I'll just have another fag." She stepped outside, took a cigarette from her pack, and lit it. Edgar watched the cloud of smoke whip away on the strong winds. He tutted. Contrary cow. He was sure she did it deliberately.

The Palmer's Reception was plastic, Edgar decided while making for the desk. The walls were adorned with artworks, mostly depicting Jack Palmer the highwayman and murderer in whose honour the hotel was named. The potted plants dotted around the black-tiled floor were fake, the marble/granite front and top of the Reception counter were equally fake and so was the insincere smile behind the receptionist's clean shaven face.

A gold-coloured badge on his lapel identified him as Geoff Vallance. Edgar judged him to be in his late thirties, slim built, clad in a badly fitting, royal blue, company issue blazer. It was the ingratiating smile that got to Edgar. He preferred people to be naturally subservient, to defer automatically to his standing as a Member of Parliament, but Geoff's whole body language was over the top. It was as if he was ready to leap over the counter, go down on his knees and polish Edgar's toecaps.

Geoff looked up and past the Honourable Gentleman. Edgar's eyes followed his gaze to the clock, which read 11:55. "Good morning, sir. How may I help you?"

Edgar's irritation rose. The toady idiot had actually checked the clock before deciding whether to wish him good morning or afternoon.

"We have reservations," he said. "Edgar Prudhoe, MP." He paused a moment to see whether his declaration would have any effect, and was delighted to see that a new respect haunted Geoff's face. "My wife, Deidre, is with me. I asked for a twin room for us. My daughter, Hannah and her fiancé, Callum McGuire will be here shortly. Make sure my daughter and McGuire are in separate rooms."

Edgar deliberately ensured his tone was peremptory, dictatorial, brooking no argument. His rural constituency was a hundred miles to the south. He had no vote catching responsibilities on the southern outskirts of York.

Geoff's hand shook slightly as he ran through a printed list of expected guests. That was what Edgar liked to see. A bit of respect translated as nervousness. Served the little snot right for his smug complacency when Edgar walked in.

"Yes, sir," Geoff said, finding and ticking off the name. "You're in two-ten, Miss Hannah Prudhoe is in two-twelve, and Mr McGuire is in two-oh-eight."

Edgar ran the arrangement through his mind. McGuire one side of them, Hann, the other, but would it be better if… "You couldn't put McGuire a couple of floors higher up?"

Geoff put on a half convincing face of apology. "I'm sorry, sir, we're full. It's Halloween, you see."

Yes and you enjoyed saying, no, didn't you, you little… Edgar snapped the thought off before it could fill his mind. "All right. It'll have to do, I suppose."

Geoff turned to his computer and hit a few keys. Studying the screen, he frowned. "We have a note here, sir, that it's your daughter's 21st birthday."

"Good grief, I almost forgot." Edgar backed off from the counter and sat down. Opening his briefcase, he took out a gift box, wrapped in celebration paper and tied with pink ribbon. Returning to the counter, he handed it over. "I want this in the hotel safe," he ordered. "It's my daughter's birthday present. A pearl necklace; and none of your junk stuff. This cost fifteen thousand pounds."

Geoff looked almost too afraid to touch it and Edgar felt another wave of satisfaction sweep through him. Smarmy little oik had probably never looked at anything more expensive than junk jewellery on the shopping channels.

"I'll attend to it the moment I print out your documentation, sir, and I'll need a credit or debit card," Geoff said. "Will you be settling bills for all three rooms, Mr Prudhoe?"

Edgar nodded and handed over his credit card. Geoff hit the computer key. Under the counter a printer buzzed like an angry wasp. While it printed out the necessary documents, Geoff took the birthday package and disappeared into the rear office. He reappeared moments later and handed a receipt over.

"That's for the safe deposit, sir," he said, and tore off the sheets of computer paper, and tucking them to one side, handed Edgar both his credit card and his room keys. Reaching across to ring the counter bell, as a porter appeared, he said, "I hope you have a pleasant stay, Mr Prudhoe."

"You'll know if we don't," Edgar warned him, and swivelled to face the exit where he could just make out his wife's umbrella. "Deidre, are you ready?"

"I'm having a smoke."

Edgar vented his annoyance on the porter. "Luggage in the Bentley. Fetch it up to two-ten, and be careful with it, lad. One scratch on it and I'll have it back out of your wage packet." He glowered at Geoff. "And it cost a damn sight more than you lot earn in a month." He marched to the door. "For crying out loud, Deidre, can we get a move on?"

***

Geoff watched Edgar fussing over the matching set of Gucci luggage as it was wheeled through the lobby, and as the lift doors closed on it and Edgar Prudhoe, he let out his breath with a hiss that took away the stress of the moment.

He stepped into the rear office where manageress, Yvonne Naylor read through her morning's emails.

Without taking her eyes off the screen, Yvonne waved in the general direction of the birthday gift Geoff had put on the corner of her desk. "You'd better get that locked away. Bad enough that we have to deal with that arrogant so and so, without taking the risk of losing his precious bloody daughter's birthday treat.

"Yes, boss."

Yvonne looked up and over the rim of her fashion glasses. "Why do I always feel that you're taking a rise when you call me boss?" Her eyes returned to the screen and the monthly returns.

Geoff did not answer right away. He picked up the gift box and shook it. A mute rattling came from within, and his head filled with images of a soft covered jewellers' box in which the expensive trinket sat.

Taking Yvonne's keys, he opened the safe, dropped it in, locked up again and put the keys back beside her left hand. That hand, shrivelled, scarred and shrunken, the index finger missing, made his skin scrawl.

Yvonne was a good looking woman. Mid-forties, slim, wide-eyed, a shower of pure blonde hair sweeping down over her shoulders, a full and proud bosom projecting above a slender waist, she was the kind of woman he would have made a play for, but that hand…

He shuddered and took the seat on the other side of the double desk from her.

Transferred in (at her own request so he understood) just a few weeks previously, she had not said how she came by the hand. Some kind of accident, according to the grapevine, and it was fairly recent. Linked to the death of her husband, it had happened in the last decade or so. Geoff wished he had known her before. The hand wouldn't have been there to put him off.

"How come you asked for a transfer here?" he had asked.

Yvonne may have thought that he was irked at her moving in above him, but that was not so. He had been with the company only four years; far too early to get his own hotel.

"I got sick of the pressure in London, especially in the reservations office. I fancied the quiet life," she had replied.

And she would get it. The Palmer sat some 10 miles south of York, on the main Hull road, and although it did well, it was rarely full. Christmas, Halloween and those times when there was a race meeting at York or Beverley. For the rest of the year, The Palmer played host only to travellers, the occasional conference, and the few holidaymakers who were too tired to make York or the coast. Yvonne was right when she said she would have a quieter life here.

Quieter, but not necessarily easier. Low staffing levels meant extra work for management, such as doubling up on Reception when the need arose; something unheard of in the larger, London establishments.

Geoff didn't mind. After the failure of his business, he was glad of the work, and the hotel trade kept him in touch with real people. He never knew when that might prove useful.

"Early check-in fee," Yvonne said and he brought his mind back to his duties.

"Come again?" he asked, his voice tinged with apology for not having paid sufficient attention in the first place.

"Prudhoe. Make sure you bill him for early check-in."

"He's an MP," Geoff reminded her.

Yvonne stopped working and concentrated on him. "I don't care if he's the Prime Minister. Check-in is two in the afternoon. He's early. Bill him."

"You think he'll pay?"

Yvonne went back to her screen. "Again, I don't care. I'm covering my backside. If he refuses to pay, head office can take it up with him. As long as I've billed him, I'm safe and so are you."

Geoff ticked the box on the Prudhoe account and the figures adjusted automatically. Returning to the bookings screen, looking at the arrivals sheet, he asked, "This crowd of old fogies from Sanford; I notice there are no special requests."

"What about it?" Yvonne asked.

"Well, don't they generally want wheelchair access, and special meals, Zimmer frame hire and stuff?"

Abandoning her work, Yvonne tutted. "I thought you used to run your own business."

He nodded. "I did."

"No wonder you went under, then, if that's the way you carried on. You should never assume anything about anyone, Geoff."

Geoff grinned. "My business going bump had nothing to do with assuming anything about anyone," he told her. "My business went bump after asset strippers decided to demolish the row of shops where I was based, and I couldn't get anywhere else… well, not at an affordable price, I couldn't. And as for making assumptions, I sold disability aids, Yvonne. It was my business to make accurate assumptions on the kinds of product the elderly and infirm might need."

"Well, now you're helping to run a hotel," she reminded him. "My information on the Sanford Third Age Club is that they're a bunch of third age rockers. Hard as bloody nails, the lot of 'em. If they'd been around when the Romans landed, Caesar would have ordered his men to turn right and tackle the Vikings instead."

Geoff smiled. "The Romans did fight the Vikings at Constantinople."

Yvonne smiled back. "No," she disagreed, displaying her own knowledge of history. "They weren't proper Romans, and the attackers weren't proper Vikings. Now let's get on with some work, huh?"

"Has anyone ever told you you're beautiful when you're so determined?"

"Flattery will get you anywhere," she countered, "but it won't get you into my pants."

Geoff smiled and concentrated on his tedious work. Thoughts rambled at the back of his mind. *If flattery won't get me into your pants, what will?* Then he remembered the hand and he shuddered.

***

Burdened with bags bearing the logos of some of the High Street's best known names, Joe felt relieved to be climbing aboard the bus for the short journey to The Palmer Hotel. He wore a thick, quilt-lined coat and strong denim jeans, but he was still wet and cold. Drops of water dripped from the peak of his cloth cap and his all-weather trainers squelched as he climbed onto the coach and began to stow the bags in the overhead racks.

"Bit wet out there, Joe," grinned Keith Lowry, the driver, a veteran of many a STAC outing.

"Stating the bleeding obvious, huh? About your mark."

"That's what I like about you: consistency. I could near as damn it set my watch by your grumbling." Keith grinned and eyed the carrier bags as Joe pressed them into the racks. "You've been shopping in Dorothy Perkins and Bon Marche?" he asked. "Is there summat we don't know about you, Joe?"

"They're not mine, you idiot. They belong to Brenda and Sheila. You know what these trips are like. They shop and I'm the bloody pack mule." Joe stripped off his coat and took a seat. "Here," he said, handing the coat to Keith. "Do me a favour and put that over your heaters."

Keith took the garment and spread it across the front of the dashboard, above the heater vents. Robbed of the warm air, the windscreen above began to mist over.

"So what's your master plan?" Joe asked settling into his seat and digging into the pockets of his cardigan for tobacco and cigarette papers.

Keith checked the time on the overhead clock at 3:55. "Assuming your lot get back on time – and if they do, it'll be a first – I drop you lot at The Palmer, take the others to The Feathers in Pocklington, and with a bit of luck, I'll be home for half past seven. I'll be back at The Feathers for ten tomorrow morning, and I should be picking you lot up at eleven. You'll be back at The Miner's in Sanford for half past twelve." He looked up into the turbulent skies. "This is also assuming nowt goes wrong. In weather like this, you never know. One high-sided lorry blown over on the motorway and your schedules are shot." He stared at Joe's cigarette. "But what I do know is you can't smoke that on my bus."

"I'm not going to," Joe retorted. "It's for when we get off."

A wave of tiredness washed over Joe. He sat back and closed his eyes for a moment. It had been a long and trying day. The weather aside, Sheila and Brenda tackled York with the same gusto they deployed on all STAC's destinations, determined to cram in as much as possible in the few hours available to them.

A lightning tour of the Minster, a wander along Shambles, where they delighted in the higgledy-piggledy arrangement of Tudor buildings, some of which were almost touching on the upper floors, and then some 'serious retail therapy' as Brenda described it, hitting every department store in town, large and small, buying skirts and tops just for the hell of it, so it seemed to Joe.

At 1:30 they had made for Betty's Tea Rooms, joining a queue which stretched out the door, along the few yards that remained of Davygate and turned the corner into Lendal. Near the front of the queue, within a yard or two of the door, Sheila and Brenda had retained fearsome grips on their umbrellas to prevent the strong winds from tearing them away, while Joe, his cap pulled low over his head and collar turned up against the October onslaught, kept up a string of complaints.

"What the hell is Betty serving with her tea and scones?" he grumbled. "LSD? Ecstasy? It must be something special to cause a queue like this."

After lunch there was more shopping, then, at 3, a call to the Jorvik Viking Centre. Looking at a model of a Viking longship in the souvenir shop, Joe commented, "Much more of this rain and we'll need the real thing."

They eventually came out at 3:40, Joe worse off to the tune of £80 which he had paid for two large Viking drinking horns. "They'll look good on the café walls," he told his companions.

Brenda had nudged Sheila. "He'll be telling everyone that the tea at the Lazy Luncheonette is good enough to make them horny."

Sheila laughed and said, "Either that or we'll have Joe telling tall tales about having hunted down the bull himself."

The blustery winds and rains compelled them to move quickly out of the centre, and hurry through Castlegate, skirting the base of Clifford's Tower, standing in splendid isolation on its mound as if still guarding the city from potential invaders, and down to the coach park on the riverside where, while the two women visited the ladies, Joe had climbed gratefully onto the coach.

"So what are you doing for the Halloween party, Joe?"

Keith's voice disturbed his sleepiness. He opened his eyes and gazed through the window. Sheila and Brenda had just come from the toilet block and were scuttling across the car park towards the coach, while the wind seemed determined to rip the umbrellas from their grasp.

"Huh?" Joe asked. "Halloween?"

"The party," Keith asked. "I thought it was fancy dress?"

"I'm going as me," Joe told him.

Keith laughed as the two women stepped onto the coach. "That should be enough to frighten off any trick or treaters."

"What should?" Brenda asked shaking her umbrella out on the step before folding it away.

"Joe turning up at the fancy dress do as himself."

Following Brenda onto the bus, Sheila shuddered. "Especially if they rattle the collecting tin under his nose." She, too, shook out her umbrella before boarding properly and joining Brenda at the seats behind Keith.

The driver laughed. "Come on, Joe, tell us."

"It's a secret," he replied.

"Don't worry, Keith," Brenda reassured him. Fishing into one of her many coat pockets, she came out with her digital camera. "We'll have all the incriminating evidence on file." She snapped a quick picture of Joe's scowling face and they laughed again.

Joe settled back and closed his eyes again. He didn't mind them poking fun at him. Only a true friend would take a rise and not mean it, and the Sanford Third Age Club were his true friends.

The club had been his idea, and the foundation upon which it stood was the unbreakable triumvirate of Sheila, Brenda and himself, each bringing their own specialist skills to their allotted roles. Many had tried to cleave a gap between them, but while they each had their own lives to lead, when it came to STAC, they were inseparable, unbreakable.

With that comforting thought, Joe drifted into a light yet much needed sleep.

***

Making her rounds, Yvonne paused at the small stage where Rick Hart and Linda Ellis were setting up their equipment.

"The Old Inn," the manageress said, handing over a key. "Make sure I get it back after the ghost walk." She watched Linda unpacking heavy duty cases, laying equipment out in order, with a practised ease that came from familiarity. "Everything all right?"

Rick held the key between the tips of his left thumb and

forefinger, and closed his right hand around it. Shuffling his hands, he held them open and they were empty. With a grin, he reached behind Yvonne's right ear and then withdrew his hand, containing the key. "Magic, y'see," he said, dropping the key in his pocket. "The view from our end is epic," Rick told her. "How about you?"

"Ignore him, Yvonne," Linda said. "He's just being a pain. We've no problems. Are we busy tonight?"

"We're expecting a large party in any time now. The Sanford Third Age Club."

Teasing cable jacks into the appropriate ports on his disco equipment, Rick, a tall, gangling, 20-something, tutted. "A bunch of little old ladies? You sure they'll stand the ghost walk?"

"My information, Rick, is that they are anything but a bunch of little old ladies. They're a mob of middle-aged, born again teenagers who drink like fish and bed hop like bed bugs, and if you cross them, you're likely to get clobbered with a bike chain."

Linda, a slim, busty brunette, whose mini-skirt bared a dangerous amount of leg, was obviously puzzled. "Bike chain?"

"It's what Teddy boys used as a weapon in the fifties," Yvonne explained. "Are you aware that tonight is also Hannah Prudhoe's 21st birthday?"

They all glanced across at the bar entrance where Edgar Prudhoe sat with Callum McGuire.

"Geoff told us when we first arrived," Rick said. "Linda'll give her the standard greeting before the show gets under way."

"Good. Make sure I get the key back after the ghost walk. I'll catch you later." With a nod, Yvonne went on her way.

Rick watched her behind wiggling away and said, "I know what I'd like to give her, and it isn't the key to the Old Inn."

Linda smiled. "Wouldn't that hand put you off?"

"Nah. Turn the lights off, I wouldn't see it."

***

23

"I'll be frank. I don't like you. I don't want you near my daughter."

Sat forward in his seat, elbows resting on his knees, hands turning a whisky glass round and round on the low, marble tiled table, Edgar did not look at Cal as he spoke. It was not that he was afraid of looking the young Scot in the eye, but he did not want to transmit their disagreement to anyone who might be taking notice.

The lounge bar of The Palmer was nowhere near full. A couple of men casually dressed with the kind of scruffiness which Edgar felt should warrant showing them the door, sat on stools at the bar, and further over, a middle-aged couple enjoyed a quiet drink. There were two members of staff behind the bar, both busy stocking up the chillers, checking the optics and other stocks, and the hotel manageress, Yvonne someone or other, was making her rounds ensuring everything was ship shape. In the corner furthest from the door, a DJ was setting up his equipment.

Edgar would have preferred more people. At least then his naturally booming voice, muted though he kept it, would have been smothered by the natural ambience. He could have also stared Cal in the eye, even if he kept a smile on his face. Duplicity of that nature came naturally to the skilled politician. And it was necessary. In this day and age, one simply never knew what kind of eavesdroppers were within earshot. Many a Westminster man or woman had learned how costly such carelessness could be, and the great unwashed liked nothing better than witnessing their political betters brought down.

He didn't, for one moment, believe that Callum McGuire would speak to the press, no matter how this little tête-à-tête turned out. Edgar had ways and means of ensuring silence, and the boy would understand by the time they were through.

"I don't see where it's up to you to like or dislike me, Mr Prudhoe. Surely it's Hann's wishes that count, and right now she wants to be with me."

"Pah." Edgar's calculated snort would leave no doubt about his feelings, but to reinforce it, he waved a dismissive hand to one side of the table as he delivered it. "She's twenty-one years old tonight. What the hell does she know about what she wants and doesn't want?"

"She's an intelligent woman, not a child," Cal argued.

"She's barely out of her gym slip," Edgar retorted, half convincing himself that such was the case. "Besides, it's not her I'm talking about. It's you." He picked up the glass and downed the whisky in a single gulp. "I'm not stupid, McGuire. I didn't get to where I am without learning to recognise subversives, and you're a bloody subversive. I know what you're after. You're worming your way into her heart to get at her money… my money. And what'll happen to it, once you have your greedy mitts on it. Every bloody penny will go to the Scots Nationalists."

Cal looked away probably to hide the fury in his eyes, Edgar decided. A fury that more than confirmed the MP's suspicions; a fury born of exposure for what he was; a fury at the accuracy with which Edgar had seen through him.

When he turned to face his girlfriend's father, Edgar's deductions were confirmed. The boy's eyes were ablaze.

"Have you listened to yourself, you idiot?" Cal demanded and a shock of anger ran through Edgar.

"Now you listen to me, lad –"

"That's the trouble, isn't it?" Cal cut in. "You want everyone to listen to you, while you ignore everything everyone else has to say. Why don't you, for once in your life, shut your mouth and open your ears. I am not a member of the Scottish Nationalists. I'm not a member of any political party. I'm not interested in politics." With each declaration, Cal jabbed his finger into the table top. "I don't want your money, I don't want your daughter's money. I want her and right now, she wants me. That's the way it is, that's the way it stays until she tells me or I tell her it's over."

Boiling with rage, Edgar glanced quickly and furtively around the room again. Keeping a fixed smile on his face, he spoke through clenched teeth. "It ends, McGuire. Tonight. I'll make it worth your while. Now here's what I want you to do…"

Cal cut in again. "Did you hear one word I said? Did you even listen to me?"

"I heard you, but I'm a man who gets what he wants, and I want you out of Hann's life."

"It's not going to happen."

"Yes it is. Now here's what you do. There's some silly bloody farce on here tonight, where they take all these silly buggers," Edgar waved at the room, "for a walk round a haunted barn at the back of this place. You'll go with them. But when they come out, you stay there. I'll come to the place at ten-fifteen. Five minutes later, you get in your car and drive away. You'll be at least ten thousand pounds better off. And you never see or contact Hann again. Get it?"

Cal glowered. "You're the one who doesn't get it. You go to the barn at ten-fifteen, but you'll be on your own." He stood. "And the only reason I'll not say anything to Hann about this is because I don't want to spoil her birthday." He stormed from the room.

Edgar noticed Yvonne Naylor's eyes on him as she made her final check of the room. He smiled obsequiously in her direction and picked up his glass to drink it off before noticing that it was already empty.

Dropping it back on the table, he, too, left the room. McGuire would be there, he knew. The temptation of ten grand would be enough to see the money-grabbing little sod turning up.

Chapter Three

"The story is not true. It was actually invented sometime in the 1970s."

Sheila's voice woke Joe. Dreaming of his flat above the Lazy Luncheonette back in Sanford, it took a moment or two for him to register his surroundings. His brain quickly translated the thrum of the dishwasher to the rumble of the bus along the A1079 out of York, and Sheila's gossipy voice soon clicked as her more formal, educational tone.

Sheila and Brenda were sat behind Keith. Joe, who normally took the jump seat across the aisle from Keith, had the double seat across the aisle to himself. Mavis Barker was keeping Cyril Peck company further down the bus. The red LED display of the coach's clock read 17:35 and even though the sun had only just set, heavy cloud, from which torrential rain still poured, ensured that darkness had already descended. The wipers flitted back and forth across the windscreen and Joe found the lights of oncoming vehicles fluid and dazzling. Weather like this reminded him of how lucky he was. Throughout his working life, he had never had to 'go out' to work. He had always lived above the café. True, when he was a young lad, before the days of daily deliveries, he had had to get out of bed and go with his father to the wholesale markets in Leeds three times a week, but back then he had always enjoyed the jaunts.

If the Sanford Third Age Club was his way of repaying something to the community that had given him so much over the years, then the café was his life. Grumpy and sour with his

27

staff and customers alike, there was still never a day when he did not want to get out of bed and open up, not a single morning when he did not feel like switching on the hotplates and ovens. It was hard work (a lot harder than many people imagined) but it made him a good living, and he enjoyed it.

His nephew, Lee, acted as the main cook these days. Clumsy and gormless he might be, but he was big and strong, yet had a delicate touch with food that Joe had never been able to match. The mainstay of the Lazy Luncheonette was the full English breakfast, bacon and sausage sandwiches, but if he was called upon to do so, Lee could turn out any meal to match the fancy restaurants head-on.

Sheila and Brenda had worked for him for over five years now. Both were widowed, both were known as part of Joe's Harem, and both were indispensable, although he would never admit it to anyone. They could run the Lazy Luncheonette just as efficiently as he could, they were unflappable, and they were so indefatigably cheerful that they provided the perfect foil to his sullenness.

Brenda had been a bank clerk before her late husband's failing health forced her to give up work. When Colin died, he left her financially comfortable, and she worked for Joe to give her something to fill the hours rather than any monetary considerations. The same could be said of Sheila. A former school secretary, when her police inspector husband, Peter, succumbed to a heart attack, she was not found wanting, but she needed fresh, more invigorating company than she had with the staff and pupils of Sanford Park Comprehensive. So she took early retirement and came to work for Joe. The two women were the best of friends, which irked Joe only at those times when he wondered whether he should date one or other of them.

He was divorced. His wife, Alison, had put up with ten years of him, and decided she wanted better than a workman's café on Doncaster Road. She walked out on him, caught a flight to the Canary Islands and Joe had heard only occasional tales of her since. In truth, the deterioration of their relationship only troubled him while they were going through it. When it was over, it was like a weight lifted from his shoulders.

"A story?" Brenda asked, bringing Joe from his reverie.

"A complete invention, according to my reading," Sheila agreed.

"What are we on about now?" Joe asked.

"Ah. The sleeping beauty's awake," Brenda teased. "Sheila was just telling me about this haunted shed at The Palmer Hotel."

Joe yawned. "Supposed to be the ghost of some highwayman, isn't it? Hanged at the gibbet in seventeen something or other."

"That's the story," Sheila agreed. "But I read up on it after we confirmed the booking. The Palmer was built in the early seventies. There's an old inn and stables building behind the hotel and they put the story about that Jack Palmer, an eighteenth century highwayman, was captured there while, er…" Sheila blushed, "let's say getting back to nature with one of the maids. The story then says he was hanged from the gibbet at Knavesmire, near where York racecourse is now sited, about 1750. In fact, the story is a complete invention, stealing from other tales from the same era."

"What tales?" Joe demanded.

"Dick Turpin for one. At the time of his arrest, he was living as *John* Palmer. There's also the legend of The Feathers, in Pocklington, where some of our people are staying tonight." Sheila jerked her head backwards to indicate their fellow club members. "According to one legend, The Feathers is haunted by the ghost of a young woman whose husband or lover was a highwayman, caught and killed in the stables behind the pub. The ghost of The Palmer is said to haunt the old inn behind the new building. According to the local historians, however, there is no report of any haunting prior to the hotel opening in 1976, but obviously, Accomplus, the group that owns The Palmer, insist that the story is a couple of centuries old."

29

"It's that kind of area, though, isn't it?" Brenda said. "York, I mean. You get ghosts of the Romans wandering through the old city. It's like Whitby and vampires, or Pendle and witchcraft. Old wives' tales."

"Like the time Joe took out his wallet and spent money?" Sheila giggled.

"Or the time you two did any work worth paying for," Joe riposted. "So what about this old pub?"

"It's behind the hotel," Sheila said, "and it's what's left of an almshouse, an inn with the stables attached. Word is they're actually nineteenth century, albeit built on the site of an earlier establishment."

"And no one lives there?" Joe asked.

Sheila shook her head. "It's an empty shell of a building, but Accomplus maintain it as a tourist attraction."

Joe shook his head sadly. "Must cost them a damn fortune," he grumbled.

"They know the value of old wives tales, Joe," said Keith from behind the wheel. "Coming up on the place now. Better get your old fogies ready."

"I'll give you old fogies one of these days," Joe clucked. He reached up and to his right and took down the PA microphone from its rest. Switching it on, he tapped the head to ensure it was working, and then announced, "Okey-dokey, folks, we're coming into The Palmer now. Those of you who are billeted here, get off, get your luggage and look sharp about it. Keith has to get the others to Pocklington before he can go home and check his lottery numbers."

"Will you still turn up to collect us tomorrow if you win, Keith?" Alec Staines called out.

"Nope," Keith replied, "but I'll send you all a postcard from Barbados."

As they cruised towards the hotel, Joe ran his sleeve over the condensation on the windows, and peered through, getting his first view of the hotel and behind it, the dark shape of the old inn.

The place itself was a five-storey glass and concrete shoebox, which could have sat comfortably amongst the office blocks of any town or city, without being noticed. It had no distinction, no character. Even the glowing, red neon sign and the pale cream walls of the front entrance said nothing about the building.

The old inn was a different matter. Lit by sparse lamps out front, and weak bulbs on its walls, it had an air of foreboding about it, augmented by a couple of jack o'lanterns hung around the door. Constructed of stone, which had been blackened by age, with a mock-Tudor front, it stood in complete isolation from the hotel and, judging by the flat, empty fields all around the area, it appeared to have been ostracised from the rest of civilisation, too. In a darkness permeated only by the thin illumination of street lamps and passing vehicles, a steeply pitched uneven roof of slate glistened in the rain, and tiny windows reflected the lights back into the night. The stables were tagged onto the far end of the inn almost as an afterthought, resembling a wooden barn, the doors sealed tight against the terrible weather.

Ghost hunting, Joe had long ago decided, was not his thing. He enjoyed puzzles, he liked pitting his wits against criminals and he revelled in the challenge of a good mystery, but he preferred them more earthbound, with the possibility of a solution. Challenging the afterlife was not, to his way of thinking, a profitable way of passing the time; the problem itself was intransigent, and any answers he found were likely to be highly subjective.

And yet, as the bus pulled up to and stopped outside the entrance, he had a feeling that this was one haunting he would enjoy taking on... if only to prove that it was no such thing.

Keith pulled a lever on his dashboard and opened the door. As always, Joe was first off the bus. He needed to be ahead to prepare the hotel for their arrival. He did not bother putting on

31

his coat, but slung it about his shoulders, pulled his cap onto his mop of curly hair, stepped down off the bus, and hurried into the reception area.

"Rotten, bloody weather," he cursed aloud as the double glass doors swung open automatically for him.

Such announcements usually attracted the attention of staff or other guests, but this time, his entrance was upstaged by an argument going on at the counter where a tall, well-dressed business type was arguing with a blonde.

"Do you know who I am?" the man demanded.

"I'm perfectly aware of who you are, Mr Prudhoe," the blonde returned, "but hotel policy makes no exception for Members of Parliament. Our check-in time –"

"I check in when I bloody well get here," Prudhoe retorted, "and I don't expect to be charged for it."

With no particular interest in politics, Joe could not place the MP, but he could see that the blonde was itching to give him a piece of her mind, even though her position made that impossible. Joe felt himself under no such restriction, but he held back on the grounds that the debate had nothing to do with him.

"Our policy is standard at all our hotels, sir," the blonde said with barely controlled restraint. "You checked in early and there is a twenty pound charge for that."

"I'll not pay," Prudhoe threatened.

"If you refuse to pay I'll have no alternative but to ask you to leave," said the blonde as Joe sidled up to the counter, "and if you then refuse to leave, I shall call the police."

Joe checked the blonde's nametag while Prudhoe launched into another tirade.

"You should think about this. By the time I'm through with your bosses, you'll be out on your ear."

"I shouldn't think so," Joe said, unable to hold himself back any longer. "She has a witness – me – to your verbal abuse."

Prudhoe rounded on him. "Mind your own bloody

business."

"You should learn some manners," Joe suggested. "And like all politicians, you should learn to shut up now and again and listen to others."

Prudhoe turned apoplectic but Joe went on undeterred.

"See, if…" Joe made a point of checking her nametag again. "If Yvonne Naylor, here, worked for me, and she didn't charge you for early check-in, she'd be in hot water. And if she insulted you or threw you out, I'd probably pay her a bonus."

Prudhoe advanced on Joe. At the same time, George Robson, a burly gardener for Sanford Borough Council entered the building.

"Hey," shouted George. "Back off, pal."

Joe smiled. "It's all right, George. The Honourable Dipstick for Moronsville South was only trying to make a point."

Prudhoe's eyes darted from Joe to Yvonne, to George and back to Joe who wondered whether the MP really was going to resort to violence. "You haven't heard the last of this," he warned Yvonne, and with a hiss, stormed off.

"I'm sorry about that, sir," Yvonne apologised.

Joe turned his attention to Yvonne. "No problem, luv. I hate guys like that, and I hated him even more when I learned he was a politician." He beamed a smile at her. "Joe Murray, Chair, Sanford Third Age Club. We've arrived."

Yvonne's face went blank for a moment and then flushed with realisation. "Oh my god, I'd almost forgotten about you. There's a bus load of you, isn't there?" She reached across and rang the desk bell to summon help, and for the first time Joe noticed her withered, deformed hand.

Her index finger was missing, the skin looked as if it had been flayed off and fresh grafted on, but the graft had never taken properly. The ugly red spread past her wrist where it began to blend with her naturally pale colour.

She noticed him looking and gave a wan smile. "An accident," she said. "I was lucky. I only lost a finger and the full use of my hand. If the fire had been much worse, I could have died.

"I'm sorry," Joe said as his members began to file in from the bus. "I didn't mean to stare."

She smiled again. "I'm used to it. Now, Mr Murray, there are, I think, sixty of you, allocated to forty rooms, and I really don't have the staff to porter for you all. If your people are prepared to wait, I can…"

"We're third age, Yvonne, not clapped out." Joe interrupted. "I can give you the full list of names. If you can just give us the keys, we'll carry our own luggage up." He leaned against the counter. "Course, if you'd rather I kicked up a fuss and threatened to report you, get you fired because I'm so important, I can oblige."

Yvonne laughed this time. "I think I can live without that."

She took the list from him as more and more members began to crowd into the lobby. Brenda pushed her way to the front.

"I've got your bag here, Joe," she said, and beamed at Yvonne. "Hello. Has Joe been moaning at you?"

"He's been very helpful as a matter of fact," Yvonne replied as Geoff Vallance appeared to lend a hand.

Brenda grinned. "Joe? Helpful? You watch yourself, luv. If he's being helpful, he's after something." Joe was about to protest when Brenda went on, "Usually a discount."

The task got under way. As Joe gave Yvonne a name, she ticked it off the list, Geoff handed over room keys and a programme of events, and the club member(s) then left. Within ten minutes, the crowd in Reception had begun to thin out, and by six o'clock, there were only Joe, Sheila and Brenda remaining.

"The Halloween party is fancy dress, isn't it?" Sheila asked taking keys for the room she and Brenda would share."

"It's not obligatory, Mrs Riley, but yes. The bar staff will be in fancy dress." Yvonne frowned. "There's a 21st birthday party in the hotel, too, and they'll be cutting into the entertainment to announce it."

Brenda sighed. "Oh to be twenty-one again, and to know how much money Joe Murray has stashed away."

"Wouldn't do you any good," Joe quipped. "I prefer older women." While Brenda tried to work out whether she had been insulted or not, Joe spoke again to Yvonne. "So who's twenty-one? Anyone we know?"

"Unfortunately, it's Hannah Prudhoe," Yvonne replied. "The MP's daughter."

"She's much more pleasant than her father," Geoff commented.

"I've seen Rottweilers more pleasant than her dad," Joe responded and took his keys.

***

"The fact remains that I am a Member of Parliament, and whether or not I'm in my own constituency, I should not be subject to such embarrassment."

Pacing the room, his mobile phone stuck to his ear, Edgar listened to the wheedling of the Accomplus flunkey.

"I know you can't be held responsible for the behaviour of other guests, but I don't blame that little snot, whoever he was. I blame your manageress, Naylor. If she hadn't been so high-handed, charging me for turning up early, there wouldn't have been an argument in the first place."

Again he paced, listening to the excuses coming from the other end. Deidre lay on the double bed, her eyes covered in a sleep mask, the phones of an mp3 player jammed into her ears; her silent way of telling Edgar she was sick of hearing him. It was the closest she came to criticism of her husband; most of the time, all he got was indifference.

"Do I need to remind you that I am a shareholder in Accomplus, and I know the Chief Executive personally? Why do you think I booked into this hellhole in the first place? As an

MP, as a shareholder, as someone who counts the CEO as an acquaintance, I expect a little special treatment when I check into one of your dumps. I don't expect to be treated the same as the other riffraff."

His temper rising, he listened again and this time he let rip with unbridled malevolence. "Either do something about it, or she's not the only one I'll be speaking to your bosses about." He slammed the phone shut and threw it on the dresser. With a glare at his wife, he strode to the bed and kicked at it.

Deidre lifted her mask and removed the earphones.

"Do something with yourself, will you? Instead of just laying there like a half drunken idiot."

***

Yvonne sighed. "Company policy is a surcharge for early check-in. I instituted company policy."

She paused and listened to the same duty manager Edgar Prudhoe had spoken to only minutes earlier. Geoff Vallance walked in and she nodded him to the seat opposite.

"If you want that charge removed from his bill," she said, "then you need to send me an email authorising it. I refuse to carry the can for that overblown mouthpiece."

She listened again. Opposite her, Geoff raised his eyebrows and pulled a sympathetic face. Yvonne shook her head at him in a gesture that said, 'I don't believe this is happening'.

"Let me make this clear," she said with insistent finality. "Unless you or someone else at Head Office authorises its removal, that charge stays on his bill, and you can threaten me with all the disciplinary action in the world, it won't make any difference." She slammed the phone down.

"Edgar Prudhoe?" Geoff asked.

Yvonne let her breath out as a hiss. "Would you believe he reported me for the early check-in surcharge?"

"I tried to warn you," Geoff reminded her. His brow knitted.

"How come he found out about it tonight and not tomorrow morning?"

"Because he came to settle the bill tonight. He wants to be away right after breakfast tomorrow. He has to be back at the Commons first thing Monday. His daughter will settle any outstanding bar bill, but he wanted to make sure the rooms were paid for so he wouldn't be, quote, 'arsing about tomorrow morning', unquote. The moment he saw the surcharge, it all hit the fan. Now I've just been told to expect a visit from the Regional Manager on Monday to assess my attitude and performance."

Geoff shook his head sympathetically. "You don't win with his kind, Yvonne. He's arrogant, ignorant, but he has contacts and he can cause you a lot of trouble. I know, believe me."

"And how do you know?" she asked.

"You remember I said my business went when the parade where I had my shop was demolished? There was a group of MPs, and Prudhoe was one of them, who put pressure on the inquiry to find in favour of the consortium that wanted to develop the site. The inquiry found in the consortium's favour and in one fell swoop created hundreds of construction jobs... while sinking a dozen small businesses. The council offered me alternative premises, naturally, but I couldn't afford the rents, so in effect, that gang of MPs put me out of business. And for what? None of the MPs lived in this area. They worked for favours. Donations to election funds, free fact-finding tours of exotic locations, tips on which companies were on the up, or prime for tearing apart. The truth came out in the end, of course, but it was rather buried in the expenses scandal. You can fight them until you're blue in the face, but you can't win."

Listening to the tale, Yvonne's features underwent several transformations, from sympathy to sorrow to anger. "I'm sorry, Geoff," she told him. "But you have to fight somewhere or these people will simply walk all over you. I see no reason why he should be treated any differently to the rest of the world." She

37

smiled. "And neither did that little chap from the Sanford Third Age Club. Murray. He gave the Honourable Gentleman some candid advice and if it came to a straight fight between them, I wouldn't back Prudhoe to win."

Geoff chuckled. "Joe Murray may be able to rattle Prudhoe's cage, but in the long run, it's the Prudhoes of this world who always run out the winners. You can't beat 'em, and you have no chance of joining them, so you do the next best thing; get on with your life and forget they exist."

Yvonne shook her head again. "Not this lady. If Prudhoe starts with me again, I'll teach him a lesson he'll never forget." She laughed. "If he survives the lesson, that is."

Chapter Four

Dressed as Morticia Addams, complete with long black wig and a skin-tight, ankle-length dress with plunging neckline, Brenda led the way into the dining room and looked around for Joe.

"That's not him dressed as Frankenstein, is it?" she asked.

Sheila's attire, a simple black dress, lent her a more conservative appearance, but white face powder and fake streaks of blood apparently dribbling from her mouth, completed a suitable picture of a vampire. The plastic fangs, however, made talking difficult and she removed them to answer her best friend.

"Too tall. Joe could only turn up as Frankenstein's little boy."

Brenda tittered as the maitre approached.

"Table for two, ladies?" he asked.

"Table for three," Sheila corrected him. "Our friend, Mr Murray, hasn't arrived yet."

Weaving his way through the tables, he showed them to an empty space by the rear wall and pulled the chairs out for them. "How will your friend be dressed, madam?" he asked.

Sheila shrugged and Brenda said, "He kept it secret, so neither of us knows."

Not everyone in the dining room had chosen fancy dress. George Robson was in his usual Saturday night suit, shirt and tie, and in the opposite corner of the dining room, Edgar Prudhoe and his party were also dressed normally if rather more grandly than most of the Sanford Third Age Club.

Many STAC members had pushed the boat out, however.

Within the Halloween theme, Cyril Peck wore a werewolf mask and alongside him, Mavis Barker sported the tall hat of a witch. Although there were a number of characters from horror movies, others had chosen different themes. Les Tanner wore the red, number one uniform of a Victorian military commander, complete with feathered hat, and his girlfriend, Sylvia Goodson was dressed as Queen Victoria herself. Alec Staines wore a double breasted, pinstripe suit and spats which, complete with his fedora, made him look like an American gangster, an image complemented by his wife's 1920s beaded overdress and cloche hat.

Settling in, declining drinks in favour of water from the carafe, Sheila and Brenda were taking in the scene around them when Darth Vader walked into the dining room. He was a good deal shorter than the actors who had appeared in the *Star Wars* movies, but the costume was accurate, right down to the fake electronic display on the chest, a pair of jackboots, and the light sabre hanging from his belt.

He drew many admiring glances as he strode into the dining hall and looked around. The maitre spoke to him, he must have replied, although hidden behind his mask, there could be no discernible movement of his lips, and it was only when the maitre pointed towards Sheila and Brenda that the women realised his identity.

"Joe," Sheila applauded as he joined them, "I would never have guessed that you could put a costume together as good as that."

Brenda chuckled. "Are you gonna work your evil magic on me later, Darth?"

Joe muttered something. His words were inaudible under the clatter of a busy dining room.

"Say that again," Brenda invited.

Joe lifted the mask onto his head and breathed out a sigh of what sounded like relief. "I said, I wish I'd never bothered. This get up is making me sweat like Brenda when she's –"

"Careful, Joe," Brenda interrupted with a warning edge in her voice.

"I was going to say making me sweat like you when you're cooking the breakfast bacon."

Joe removed the mask altogether and as his cape spread out, they could see he wore his favourite, pale green, fisherman's gilet underneath it.

Registering their disapproval, Joe went on the defensive. "I need the pocket space for my tobacco and lighters."

"Darth Vader doesn't smoke," Sheila scolded.

"He'd melt his mask if he tried," Brenda agreed.

"He'd also know how to deal with you two," Joe protested and removed his mask altogether, hanging it by its elastic straps over his chair. He made a two-handed motion of wringing a neck. "You'd either do as you're told or he'd throttle the pair of you. And you'd have to bow to me."

He swept his torch/light sabre to one side and it clattered against the pocket of his gilet.

"Joe?"

"Yes, Brenda?"

"You're rattling."

"Shut your rattle," Sheila ordered.

He chuckled. "Tobacco and lighter," he explained and reached into the large, deep pockets of his gilet to remove his tobacco tin and his brass, engraved Zippo lighter. Putting them on the table, close to his elbow, he looked around the room. "Good turnout. I see our people have entered into the spirit of the thing."

"And none more than you, Joe." Sheila frowned. "But not that MP and his party. Snooty sod."

"A snapper, too," Joe agreed.

Sheila stood. "Something to eat, I think. Shall I pick something for you, Joe, or would you like to help yourself?"

"I'll wait," he said, eyeing the wine waiter. "You want a drink?"

"House white," Brenda suggested and accompanied Sheila to the self-service carvery.

Joe secured a bottle of wine from a passing waiter and poured two large glasses for Sheila and Brenda and a small one for himself.

"You know me," he said when they returned with plates of food. "I'd rather have Guinness than Chateau Plonk."

While they sat, he made for the carvery and returned a few minutes later with a plate of roast chicken, potatoes and various vegetables. As he began to work on his meal, a busty young brunette dressed in a tiny lemon top and white mini-skirt, swept past them, bestowing a friendly smile on Brenda. She wove her way through the tables, to the coffee dispenser, turned, faced the diners, and brought a radio mike to her lips.

"Ladies and gentlemen, I'd just like to introduce myself. I'm Linda Ellis, your DJ for the first half of tonight's entertainment here at The Palmer, and I'd like to run through tonight's programme for you, but please carry on and enjoy your meals as I tell you what we have in store for the evening."

Joe tutted and knocked his lighter to the floor. "No finesse," he said, bending to pick up the lighter and drop it into the right hand pocket of his gilet. "Fancy coming out with this kind of announcement during dinner."

His two friends hushed him.

"I'll be running the disco from nine until about ten o'clock, and then for those of you who dare, we'll take our ghost walk through the old inn and stables," Linda said. "If you're of a nervous disposition or if you're bad on your pins, I wouldn't recommend it, but if you fancy yourself as York's answer to The Ghostbusters, then come with me and experience at first hand, the spooky goings-on in the old building. After the ghost walk, we're back here in the bar, where my partner, the fabulous Rick Hart, will steer you through an hour of karaoke, then it's the fancy dress parade, with great prizes for the winners, and after that we're dancing the night away through the witching hour until one in the morning."

Linda paused and stared around the room as if assessing the extent to which she'd got her message across.

"So that's disco at nine, ghost walk at ten, karaoke from eleven, fancy dress parade at eleven forty-five, and then disco until one. Enjoy your meals and I'll see you all later in the bar."

As Linda switched off the mike and made her way from the dining room, she was waylaid by Edgar Prudhoe.

Brenda said, "Ooh, Joe, you must be up for a prize in that fancy dress parade."

With one eye on Linda and Edgar, who appeared to be exchanging stern if not harsh words, Joe snorted. "Really looking forward to it... not."

Sheila tried to encourage him. "Come on, Joe. You must have worked really hard on that outfit."

He shook his head. "I made the chest piece from some old bits of coloured bathroom tiles, the light sabre is an old torch, I hired the cape from Sanford Theatrical Costumes on Market Street, borrowed the riding boots from a niece and the mask I bought on a day trip to Blackpool about ten years ago. The only hard work I put into it was getting the damn stuff on."

"It's still worth a prize," Brenda said.

"Have you seen the prizes?" he demanded while watching Linda hurry from the room, her features blazing. "The winner gets a voucher for an overnight stay in any of Accomplus's hotels, and even that has conditions attached to it. The room is free, but you have to pay for dinner and breakfast. The two runners up tonight get free drinks at the bar. Prizes? They can shove 'em."

***

Rick's fingers danced over his control board, and lights flickered on and off according to the switches activated. With the music muted into headphones laid to one side, he watched

43

the multicoloured lights pick up the backbeat and, satisfied that everything was working as it should, he stopped the music.

Linda hurried in, her face flushed and worried.

"What's wrong, sugar?" Rick asked.

"That… that… *arse!*"

Rick grinned. "You turn me on when you're angry. Which arse are we talking about?"

"Edgar, do-you-know-I'm-a-Member-of-Parliament, Prudhoe. He just checked to make sure we're going to announce his daughter's birthday, I said yes, and then he told me to make sure we do it properly or I'll likely lose my job."

Now Rick laughed. "Did you tell him you don't work for The Palmer?"

"Course I did," Linda replied. "He told me if I didn't watch my mouth, he'd make sure I never got another gig here. Someone should teach that ignorant sod a lesson."

"Maybe I'll haunt him after the disco." Rick held his arms up, the hands forward, half clenched like claws, and matched the gesture with a twisted face.

"Idiot," Linda said and half-smiled. "You set up for the old inn?"

"Yep," Rick nodded. "Have you spotted a mark?"

"There's a middle aged guy dressed as Darth Vader," Linda told him. "I saw him just now in the dining room. He's wearing some kind of zip-up body warmer under his costume. And he owns a brass cigarette lighter. Looks like a Zippo, but it could be a fake. He had it on the table near his elbow until he knocked it off. Berk."

"If he's wearing a cape, it could be difficult," Rick murmured.

"Rick," Linda pointed out," it's hammering down out there. If he tries to go out in a cape, he'll take off." She laughed. "He'll end up flying over York like Batman."

"It's Superman that flies," Rick grinned.

"You know what I mean," Linda pouted. "I'll be suggesting they put on warmer clothing. That guy will have a smoke before we go in. I know his type. I'll keep an eye on which pocket he drops the lighter in, and signal you. All right?"

"No sweat," Rick agreed. "Anyone else?"

"Some old codger dressed as the Duke of Wellington," Linda replied. "Fancy silver pen in his top pocket." She patted herself just above the left breast. "Should be easy enough."

"With this on?" Rick held up a complex headset attached to which was what appeared to be a camcorder, but was in fact an electronic monocular. "I'll pinch your knickers in the dark and you won't know about it until the draught whistles in."

Linda disapproved with a pout. "I can't believe you paid three hundred pounds for that."

"And I can't believe you'd be prepared to let me break my neck in the pitch dark without it." Rick gave an insane little laugh. "While I'm wearing this, I'll nick the Duke's wallet if you like."

She shook her head. "Haven't seen where he keeps his wallet. Same goes for Darth Vader. Just concentrate on the pen and the lighter."

"They're as good as mine."

***

"Our friendly, neighbourhood parliamentary thug is creating a lot of trouble," Geoff said.

Signing off the day's returns and dropping them into a large envelope for dispatch to Accomplus's London HQ, Yvonne asked, "What has he done now?"

"Not what. Who. Linda Ellis," Geoff replied, and smiled. "I don't mean done her. That sounds a bit naughty. He's certainly upset her. Threatened to get her contract cut off at the cheque book if she doesn't watch her tongue."

Yvonne clucked. "He really is an annoying pain in the…" She trailed off as the Reception bell rang.

"I'll get it," Geoff said and left the rear office to find Edgar

45

stood at the counter. "Yes, Mr Prudhoe, how may I help you?"

"I left a birthday gift in your safe earlier," Edgar announced. "I'd like it back."

"Of course, sir." Geoff turned again for the office.

"Come on, lad. Look sharp. Haven't all night to stand around here."

Disregarding the bombast, Geoff ambled into the office, took Yvonne's keys from beside her gnarled left hand, opened the safe, and retrieved the package. Placing the keys back on her desk, he buried his squeamishness and studied her malformed hand. "Does it hurt?"

Yvonne looked up into his eyes, then followed their gaze down to her hand, and then looked back up again with a wan smile. "Not anymore. Agony when it first happened, excruciating when they took the index finger and then tried to correct the deformity, more pain when the skin grafts didn't take properly, but these days it's only the memory that hurts."

"You must tell me about it."

Again she smiled. "One day."

Geoff picked up the safe deposit receipt book, then moved back to Reception.

"Where the hell have you been?" Prudhoe demanded. "The vaults of the Bank of England?"

"There are certain security procedures we have to follow, sir," Geoff told him and opened the receipt book at the appropriate page. "If you could sign to say that you've received your property."

Edgar picked up a hotel pen. "I'll sign as unexamined," he said.

Geoff was surprised. "No one has tampered with it, Mr Prudhoe. You can see that for yourself."

"I can't see anything of the kind, lad. I can see that it looks like it did when I handed it over, but how do I know you haven't opened it, taken a look inside, and parcelled it up again. I'll sign for it unexamined." He scribbled his signature on the docket. "You know, your kind and the blonde bimbo who works with you are entirely symptomatic of what's wrong with this country. If you knew how to do an honest day's hard work we'd all be better off."

Snatching up his package, Edgar turned to walk away and his eyes met Joe's. Standing by the dining hall entrance, Joe refused to be out-stared, and Edgar marched briskly into the bar. As his back disappeared, Joe, in the act of rolling a cigarette, approached Reception.

"I'm sorry, sir," Geoff said, "but you can't smoke that in here."

"Not going to," Joe told him. "Tell me something, why do you put up with that kind of abuse?"

Geoff shrugged. "It goes with the job, Mr Murray. I'm not allowed to answer back."

Joe grunted. "I run a café. If he came in there and spoke to me the way I just heard him speak to you, I'd have my nephew throw him head first into the chip fat."

Geoff smiled at the imagery. "Your nephew."

"Lee Murray," Joe explained. "Played prop for the Sanford Bulls until someone kicked his kneecap in. Big bugger, you know. He'd eat Prudhoe for breakfast and pick his teeth with the bones."

Again Geoff smiled. "I'd probably pay to watch, sir, and I'm sure my manageress would, too, considering the trouble he's caused her."

"I was here," Joe said.

"Was there anything I can help you with, sir?" Geoff asked bringing the conversation back to business.

"No. Just passing the time of day. I'll see you later, son."

***

The rain was still falling, driven by powerful gusts of wind, when Joe stepped out through the front entrance and sheltered

47

under the portico. Across from him, an umbrella propped against her shoulder, Deidre Prudhoe drew on a cigarette.

Joe lit his hand rolled smoke and said, "Never gives up, huh? The weather."

"Making up for the roasting summer," she replied. She eyed his Darth Vader get up. "You're hoping for one of the big prizes?"

He laughed. "No. Just showing off. I put this lot together weeks ago and I didn't even know there was a prize." He offered his hand. "Joe Murray."

She shook it. "Deidre Prudhoe."

Although he knew who she was, Joe pretended not to. "Oh, you're the MP's wife." He chuckled. "Good job I wasn't slagging him off, huh?"

Deidre pulled on her cigarette and then watched the wind whip the smoke away as she exhaled. "I'm used to it. I try not to get involved."

"I run my own business," Joe told her. "A café in Sanford. I meet a lotta different people, and you know, most of the time when I meet someone who goes out of their way to, shall we say, trample on other people, it's a defence mechanism."

Deidre grinned. "Attack before someone attacks you? Not in Edgar's case. He really is as obnoxious as he pretends."

Joe frowned. "Unusual."

"What is?"

"Hearing a wife who's been married for so long talk like that about her husband."

Now she frowned, too. "How do you know how long I've been married? Are you a reporter?"

"Nope. I really do run a café in Sanford, but I'm also a bit of a private detective, and I deduced it," he told her with a broad smile. "It's not difficult. Today is your daughter's twenty-first birthday. She looks like a younger version of you, therefore she must be your daughter and not your stepdaughter. Edgar Prudhoe is an intelligent man, despite his bluster, and he wouldn't have, let's say, 'got you into trouble' prior to marrying you. That would compromise his reputation and his reputation must be valuable to him or he wouldn't keep saying, 'do you know who I am'. It's reasonable to assume then, that you were married before your little girl came along, and that means you've been married for more than 21 years."

Crushing out her cigarette, Deidre fumbled in her pocket. Joe watched as she swapped hands on the umbrella and fumbled in the other pocket, before coming out with her cigarettes. She took one from the pack, lit it and then dropped the pack back in her right hand pocket before changing her mind, taking it out again and putting it in the left. At the conclusion of this performance, she said, "Very clever. But how do you know Hannah isn't my daughter from another marriage and Edgar married me on the rebound?"

"Possible but unlikely," Joe declared. "He lodged a birthday gift with Reception and judging by the snippet of conversation I overheard, it was quite valuable. Would a man lavish such a gift on a child that was not his own? I know I wouldn't. Like I say, possible. But unlikely."

Allowing the cigarette to dangle from her lips, Deidre gave him a small round of applause. "You're clever, Mr Murray," she said, dragging on her smoke again. "Very clever. And spot on. Edgar and I have been married for 23 years."

"Which doesn't go to explaining how you could, er, run your husband down to a complete stranger," Joe said, gratified by her admiration.

"Complete strangers are the best people to run him down to." She laughed. "As long as they don't work for the Sunday papers. Edgar is a good husband, in the sense that he is a good provider. But he's also ambitious. He's been an MP for eight years, and he's determined that one day, he will be in the driving seat at Number Ten. The trouble is, he's also as thick as the proverbial short plank. It hasn't dawned on him why he's been on the back benches for eight years. He was overlooked in the shadow cabinet and when the party came to power, he didn't even get a junior post. He thinks it's because the Prime Minister is waiting to call another election, at which Edgar is certain they will win with a clear majority, and then he'll land a decent job in government."

"You don't believe that?"

"I do not," she assured him. "Most of his parliamentary colleagues can't stand him. He's too noisy, too brash, and if you've been listening in on his conversations, you'll realise he's too self-centred." Deidre puffed her cigarette again. "You're a businessman. How do you stay in business?"

Joe shrugged. "I give my customers what they want at a reasonable price."

"Exactly," Deidre agreed. "Edgar gives his constituents what they want, a dedicated member who will look after their interests. But that's all. Away from the constituency, he bullies people who stand in his way. The voters in the constituency don't care about that because they don't see it, but the parliamentarians are a different breed. They see a man who is prepared to push himself, not the needs of the country."

"I thought all politicians were like that," Joe commented.

"Not so," Deidre argued. "Most go into politics from a genuine desire to see the country improved."

"You should try telling that to the redundant miners of Sanford," Joe grumbled. Before she could react, he asked, "And none of this troubles you?"

Deidre pulled in a large lungful of smoke and let it out with a loud hiss. It escaped into the night like a will o' the wisp, stolen away by the powerful winds. "Like I said, he's a good provider."

Joe crushed out his cigarette on the stubber. "I was a good provider, too, but it didn't stop my wife clearing off to Tenerife when she'd had enough." He turned and walked back into the hotel.

***

The beat of *The Monster Mash* faded away and while Linda picked up the microphone, couples drifted off the dance floor.

"I enjoyed that," said Brenda, as she and Sheila rejoined Joe at a window table. "Haven't heard it for years."

"A bit obvious, wasn't it, Joe?" Sheila asked.

"For Halloween, practically obligatory," he replied, taking a wet from a glass of bitter. "There are other, spookier pieces she could have picked."

"Name one," Brenda challenged with a naughty gleam in her eye.

Joe thought about it for a moment. "*Still I'm Sad*, The Yardbirds," he said. "Not exactly ghostly, but quite haunting. Or *See Emily Play*, by Pink Floyd. Seriously bizarre." He thought again for a moment. "And what about *Johnny Remember Me*? That was a ghost in the wind."

"Offside, too," Sheila said. "None of them had anything to do with Halloween."

"You have to think laterally," Joe told her and as Linda began to speak, he concentrated on her.

"Right, ladies and gentlemen, that was *The Monster Mash* getting us into the creepy mood for Halloween." Linda raised her voice a little. "Are you having fun?"

Her question was greeted with a half-hearted chorus of, "Yes."

"I can't hear you." She raised her voice further. "Are you having fun?"

The chorus this time was louder.

"Ooh, you're hard work, you lot." She glanced down at her prompts. "All right before we go any further, ladies and gentlemen, we have a birthday at The Palmer tonight. Not only a birthday, but a twenty-first birthday." She giggled. "Oh to be twenty-one again and know what I know now." She waited for the laughter and when it did not come, she repeated, "Told you; you're hard work. All right, let's all wish a happy twenty-first

51

birthday to Hannah Prudhoe."

Starting the music, Linda led the applause and the singing of *Happy Birthday to You,* while Hannah Prudhoe stood at her table and blushed.

"False modesty," Joe denounced.

"Huh?" Sheila asked.

"That blush. If she's anything like her old man and old lady, she's never blushed in her life."

***

At the Prudhoes' table, Edgar, Deidre and Cal applauded Hann as she sat down again. A cake arrived from the kitchens, sparklers crackling away on its top layer of icing. Eager to be of service, Geoff Vallance lit candles either side of the sparklers, then retired discreetly to the bar entrance from where he could watch the proceedings while keeping an eye on Reception.

"Prezzie time," Deidre said. "You go first, Callum."

Cal dipped into his pocket and came out with a small gift box. He handed it over with a kiss, and Hann tore at the wrapping. Inside was a ring box. She opened it on a band of white gold with a cluster of tiny ice diamonds.

"I was going to ask your permission, Edgar, but now that Hann is over the age of consent…" he turned on her. "Will you?"

She slipped the engagement ring on her finger, admired it for a moment, then threw her arms around his neck and kissed him.

Edgar looked on, his face betraying thunder, but when Hann's eyes travelled back to him, he forced a smile of paternal indulgence.

Deidre was next, passing her daughter a soft, floppy parcel. Again Hann tore it open and came out with a Pashmina shawl in white. Hann was beside herself with delight, and hugged and kissed her mother.

Finally, Edgar handed over his gift box. "A very special gift for a very special girl on a very special birthday," he announced.

Hann rattled the box against her ear. "I'm almost too nervous to open it, Daddy," she said.

Beaming a doting smile upon her, Edgar said nothing.

Carefully, as thought she did not want to damage it, Hann teased open the bow in the ribbon and lay it to one side on the table. Then she picked apart the creased folds of the wrapping paper and lay that flat on the table, too.

Inside was a red velvet covered necklace case. Her hands trembling she lifted it and prised it open. A frown creased her brow.

"Daddy, is this a joke or something?"

The smile wiped from Edgar's face. "What?"

Hann turned the box to show them. "It's empty."

Chapter Five

Joe hurried through to Reception and rapped the bell.

He could hear voices coming from the back office... correction: he could hear one voice coming from the back office. Edgar Prudhoe was making his feelings plain.

On the revelation of the empty trinket box, he had brought proceedings in the bar to a halt with a roar that drowned out the music. Linda had stopped the track and silence had fallen over the room. And through that silence, Edgar's voice had come as the bellow of rage which would have befitted many of the ghouls, ghosts and monsters depicted in the room.

"Some thieving bastard is going to pay for this," he screamed. Catching sight of Geoff at the bar entrance, he ordered, "Lock all the doors. No one leaves this building until everyone has been searched."

While he stormed from the room, Geoff following, flapping in his wake, Joe crossed to the Prudhoes' table and asked what was going on.

Hann was in a flood of tears and incapable of answering, Deidre was intent upon her cocktail, a vodka and orange if Joe was not mistaken, and it was left to Cal to lift up the jewel case and show it to Joe.

"Someone's stolen it," Cal said.

"Stolen what?" Joe demanded.

"A pearl necklace," Deidre mumbled. "It was Hann's birthday present from Edgar."

"Expensive?" Joe asked.

Deidre turned dull eyes on him, a sharp contrast to the life he had seen in them when they were smoking outside the main entrance. "Fifteen thousand," she told him. She sounded drunk, too.

Joe whistled. "Fifteen gr... Does your husband have more money than sense?"

A flash of anger crossed her face, but Cal diverted attention. "It's been in the hotel safe all day. How can anyone have nicked it?"

"I know it has," Joe replied. "I saw him get it back earlier. Excuse me, will you."

At that point, he returned to Sheila and Brenda, sat over by the wall near the entrance, and divested his Darth Vader cape, and homemade breastplate and light sabre. "Look after these, will you," he said, and marched out.

Waiting at Reception while Edgar continued to rant, his voice audible, the individual words incomprehensible through the closed door, Joe ran through the possible scenarios. There were not many that made sense and the courses of action open to Prudhoe and The Palmer were limited and precarious, especially...

He rattled the bell again, more urgently. The office door opened and Geoff stepped out, closing it behind him. For the brief instant that it was open, Joe heard Prudhoe scream, "I'll sue the lot of you."

"Yes, Mr Murray," Geoff asked. "How may I help you?"

"You can cut the robot speech for a start," Joe replied. "You're not on one of your company training courses, so you don't have to behave like a pre-programmed cyborg. And you can't help me," he went on before Geoff could protest, "but I can help you. I need to speak to you, your boss, Yvonne wossname, and Prudhoe. Now."

"I'm sorry, sir, but Mrs Naylor is tied up and I doubt that Mr Prudhoe –"

"Cut the crap," Joe interrupted. "If loudmouth in there ever wants to see his necklace again, then he needs to talk to me."

Geoff's eyebrows rose.

"I'm the best damned detective in this part of the world," Joe said, "but before I can start work I need to see him. Now let me in there."

"If you'd like to wait, Mr Murray, I'll just –"

Joe interrupted again. "No. Don't ask his permission. A control freak like that will only give you the bum's rush. Just let me in there."

Geoff still appeared doubtful.

"Look, son, I'll take full responsibility. At the absolute worst I may create the need for a by-election in whichever constituency he represents, but no blame will attach itself to you or this hotel."

"Well the trouble is, sir…"

Joe snapped. "Stop sitting on the fence and following the company line. Let me get in to speak to Prudhoe. If you don't, you, your boss and the hotel group could end up carrying the can for one person's actions." He moved to the side of Reception where a part of the counter could be lifted to permit access.

Geoff hovered on the edge of indecisiveness. Joe fastened eye contact, and Geoff backed down, lifting the counter section to let Joe in.

He hurried through and into the office where Prudhoe sat reading the riot act to Yvonne, and threatening reprisals on a biblical scale.

Whipping his head round to face Joe, he snapped. "Get out."

Ignoring him, Joe pulled up a chair and sat to one side between Prudhoe and Yvonne. Geoff hovered in the background by the door, one ear cocked for the Reception bell.

"Did you hear me?" Prudhoe yelled. "I said get out."

Joe took out his tobacco tin and made a great show of rolling a cigarette.

Prudhoe rose to his feet. "Are you deaf or just plain stupid? Get out before I throw you out."

Joe ran his tongue along the gummed edge of the cigarette paper, and completed the cigarette. Dropping it into his shirt pocket, he put the lid back on his tin and dropped that into his side pocket. Only then did he look at Prudhoe, and as he did so, he pointed at Geoff.

"You see him? He has a black belt in karate. I know because instead of passing the day shouting the odds at him, I took time to speak to him. You make one silly move, Prudhoe, and he will floor you. He will then restrain you until the police arrive, when I will insist they charge you with assault."

Prudhoe's mouth fell open. He half turned to look at Geoff who maintained his air of subservience. Prudhoe glanced back at Joe.

"That's better," Joe said. "Now sit down, shut your mouth and let's see what we can sort out."

Yvonne worked hard to suppress her amusement. "I'm sorry, Mr Murray, but Mr Prudhoe is right. This affair has nothing to do with you."

"No? Let's see about that, huh? Five minutes ago, Prudhoe stood up in the bar and demanded that you lock all the doors until everyone has been searched. Now you tell me, what right have you, or he, to invade my privacy with an illegal body search? It could be an offence under the Human Rights Act." As Joe went on, Yvonne's face paled. "Secondly, if you choose to lock all the doors, or man them with security officers to prevent people leaving, then it becomes false imprisonment, another offence in common law and under the Human Rights Act. I'm only talking about me but I have sixty of my members out there, all of whom will take the same line. Do you still insist it has nothing to do with me, Ms Naylor?"

Risking a glance at Prudhoe, he realised Yvonne was not the only one worried by his fanciful scenario.

Prudhoe, however, was more vocal than the manager. "I've been robbed."

"You have," Joe agreed, "but that does not give you the

57

authority to trample over the rights of others. You're perfectly entitled to call the cops. At least your insurance would be valid if you did, but it makes more sense to carry out discreet inquiries before we go that far." Joe grinned. "And as it happens, you have Yorkshire's best detective right in your midst."

Yvonne frowned; Geoff frowned. Prudhoe frowned too. "Who?" he asked.

"Me," Joe said with great affront. "Hercules Porridge has nothing on me. Miss Marbles is an amateur, and I wouldn't give Sherlock Bones house room. I've investigated and solved more crimes like this than you've made speeches in the Commons. There's every chance, Prudhoe, that we can find your missing necklace and nick the thief, but only if you stop your screaming and carrying on, and start talking to people; particularly me."

"Do you know who I am?" Prudhoe raged.

Joe invested as much cynicism into his reply as he could muster. "We all know who you are because you've done nothing but remind everyone since you got here. For once, you're going to have to stop talking and start listening, and speak only when you're spoken to, and, God help us, answer a question directly instead of trying to put some spin on it."

An uneasy silence fell.

Yvonne broke it. "Are you sure you can help, Mr Murray?"

He nodded. "I'm always sure I can help, but that doesn't mean to say I can crack the problem. If I can't, you'll know within half an hour. Either way, we'll need to call the cops within the next hour or so. Even if I can pinpoint the thief, you'll need the law here to arrest him." Joe swung on the politician. "Do you want this necklace back?"

"It cost fifteen thousand pounds."

Joe tutted. "What did I tell you about giving straight answers? I didn't ask how much it cost, I asked if you want it back."

Prudhoe took a deep breath. "Well of course I bloody do."

"Then we talk. I'm going to step outside for a smoke. While

I'm gone, you need to think about everything that's happened here today. Because when I come back in, I need to know it all."

Yvonne half rose. "I'd better get Linda and her partner to put an end to the entertainment."

"No," Joe insisted. "Let it go ahead. Let the ghost walk go on as it should have done."

Prudhoe was appalled. "What? And while you lot troop off round that old shed, the thief can do a runner with my necklace. Not ruddy likely."

"That is precisely why the programme needs to go on," Joe insisted. "Look, I've just pointed out that if you try to keep people walled up or you try to search them, you're leaving yourself and the hotel wide open to legal action. Now think about this, Prudhoe. Someone in this hotel has that necklace in his pocket. While that is the case, he's on pins. What's his best chance of getting away? While we're all playing ghost hunters round the old building, he can run for it. But he won't get far. We can have people on the lookout for him. And even if he gets away, he still won't get far because we'll know who he is. He won't get to York or Hull before we have every cop in the country looking for him."

Yvonne nodded. "It makes sense."

"All right, Murray," Prudhoe agreed. "We play it your way." He checked the time. "It's nine thirty. If you don't have anything by the time the ghost walk is up, we call the police."

Joe stood up. "Deal. I'll be five minutes."

***

In the Old Inn, Rick strung up the last of his temporary lights, attaching it to a fake oil lantern above the bar. Climbing off his stepladder, he stood back to admire his handiwork. Eight bulbs spread about the room, all wired back to a remote-operated isolator, which in turn was hooked into a heavy duty truck battery.

He and Linda had covered this gig once a month for the last year and a half, and he'd always maintained that securing The Palmer's agreement had been a skilled piece of creative salesmanship on Linda's part, coupled to a skilled piece of artistic creativity on his.

It was, as Linda always complained, a long journey… well, long-ish. Bradford lay about 30 miles east of York and after wrap up, about one in the morning, it would be two before they climbed into the van for the journey home, and getting for three before they stepped into their shared apartment in the Wibsey area.

And he, too, often wondered whether it was worth it. By the time they'd paid for fuel, meals and drinks, they would be lucky to clear £100 on the night. Not a lot by 21st century standards. He'd be willing to bet that most of the oldies from the Sanford Third Age Club made more from their pensions, and they didn't have to work for it.

But beggars could not be choosers and the gig was fun if nothing else. The hard work came with the setup; stringing up the lights, running the wires discreetly across the fake oak beams of the ceiling, and hooking them into an LED sensor pad which hung around the real light switches just behind the door. When Linda led the punters in, she would reach up to the switches as if she were turning them on, but in fact, Rick would operate the lights from his hidey hole, a cupboard at the side of the old bar, in plain view of everyone.

When that was done, he got to lay low here in the Old Inn for half an hour or so, and when the punters were in, listening to Linda telling them the tale of Jack Palmer, Rick would switch off the lights for one minute.

Only during those 60 or so seconds when the lights were out did he have any *skilled* work to do. He had to move fast. Out of his hidey hole, rush amongst the crowd, touch one or two people, dip a couple of pockets, and back into his cupboard to switch the lights back on.

Not only fast, but silent, too. He couldn't afford to make a single sound. He had to control his breathing so that even the most acute hearing could not detect his presence. He wore no aftershave or other fragrances to eliminate any possibility of anyone guessing that he was the 'ghost' of the Old Inn. All a bit awkward now that his trainers were wet and squelching with every step.

Everyone knew it was him, obviously. When he turned up for the second half of the evening and 'found' the missing property in various places around the bar, they all guessed that he had taken them, but the warm applause which greeted the end of the act told him that the punters took it all in good part.

He'd grabbed some serious goodies in his time, too. He picked one guy's wallet and it contained hundreds of pounds. Tempting. He'd wondered idly whether the man would miss the odd ten or twenty. But Linda had always impressed upon him the need for absolute honesty. His conjuring skills, his startling ability to pick pockets, saw them with a steady and above all, *honest* income. Not enough, granted, but then, there was never enough money coming in. But at least, he thought as he squelched over to the cupboard at the side of the old bar, it was honest.

He checked the cupboard door, swishing it back and forth to ensure that the hinges did not creak. Linda's patter, which she delivered skilfully even with the lights out, would ensure that the soft click of the catch was masked, but he didn't want that door creaking.

Satisfied that it was fine, he shut himself inside, and then placed his eye to the hole he had drilled in the door a year and a half previously. It was set to give him a view of both the area where the punters would stand, and the LED sensor that would kill and re-ignite the light. In order to test it, he aimed the infrared control through his spy-hole and pressed it. The room and his cupboard were plunged into unimaginable blackness. Dropping his night vision lens into place, he checked that, too, throwing open the cupboard door and staring round. Satisfied, he checked his watch (non-luminous, obviously). Twenty minutes to go before Linda dragged them out of the bar.

Now how was he going to stop his feet from squelching?

***

"So tell me about this necklace," Joe invited.

Prudhoe grunted but as he began to describe, they could sense the ring of hubris and pride in his voice. "Eighteen inch, double knotted, fine silk thread, South Sea cultured pearls, twelve to sixteen millimetre. Quadruple A shape, which means they are near perfect spheres, triple A body and lustre. Not exactly perfect, but the body and shape are near as damn it. Nacre, that's a measurement of the thickness of the pearl coating, is quadruple A. You can't get better. The clasp is a white gold and four-diamond Buckingham. Necklace, fourteen thousand pounds and change, clasp six hundred pounds and change, complete with a couple of matching earrings, the lot comes to a shade over fifteen thousand pounds." He jabbed an angry finger into the desk. "And I want them back."

"Chill out, Prudhoe. We have to try to build up a picture of what happened before we think about getting the necklace back. Can I ask where you got them?"

"None of your damned business," Prudhoe returned.

Joe fumed a moment. "All right. Who put the birthday wrapping on them?"

"The shop where I bought them," Prudhoe replied with a note of surprise in his voice. It was as if he expected Joe to know the answer.

"Next question," Joe said. "Did you actually see them packaged up?"

The MP frowned. "I don't understand. I was there. Of course I was."

"Sure you were," Joe agreed, "but did they parcel the things up for you there and then on the counter, or did they take them into the backroom and do it?"

"No. They… are you suggesting they were never even in the box?" Prudhoe's face became suffused again. "What do you take me for, Murray? An idiot? I'm a member of parliament. I only deal with reliable companies."

"You're also a human being," Joe retorted. "You wouldn't be the first to walk away from a shop with a steak and kidney pie only to learn that it was a doctored sausage roll when you got home." He took out his tobacco tin again. "We don't have long, Prudhoe, and I want to get through as much as we can so I can go on this ghost walk. I want to be there to see what, if anything, happens. Before then, we need to investigate every possible avenue, and we start at the logical place. If you never saw the necklace, how do you know it was in there to begin with?"

Prudhoe's back stiffened under Joe's tirade. "I trust the seller," he said.

"All right." Joe swung on Yvonne. "You took the package from Prudhoe when he arrived this morning."

"No. Geoff did." Yvonne nodded at her assistant. "But I saw him put it in the safe."

"How many people know the combination to the safe?" Joe asked.

Yvonne held up the keys. "There is no combination."

Joe remained unabashed. "How many keys are there?"

"Four," Yvonne replied. "Three are kept here on the premises, the fourth is at Head Office in London."

"I notice you're not telling us where they are," Prudhoe said.

"Security procedures, sir," Geoff reported from the doorway. "The only persons who are aware of the keys' locations are Yvonne and myself and our opposite numbers on the other shift."

"Security procedures can be breached," Joe pointed out. "How many times during the day has this office been left unattended?"

Yvonne pursed her lips. "A good number, I should imagine, but the office is locked up at all times when it's unattended. Mr Murray, the chances of anyone getting in here, getting the safe open, taking that package, removing the contents, and putting everything back are so remote they're almost impossible."

"Almost but not entirely," Joe replied. He spread a line of tobacco along his cigarette paper and rolled it up. "To someone well-prepared, it may be difficult, but it's not impossible." Before Prudhoe could bring up another smug protest, Joe rounded on him. "In the same way, just because a seller has never ripped you off before, doesn't mean he didn't do so this time." He paused to let the message sink in. "So, you took the package back before you went into the bar. Where did you keep it?"

"It was in my briefcase, beneath the table," Prudhoe said. "In fact it was the sole reason I took the briefcase with me. I don't normally carry one on a night out."

"The briefcase was locked?" Joe wanted to know.

"No."

"Was it left unattended at any time?"

"No."

"You're sure of that? For instance, when you and your daughter's boyfriend went to the bar, your wife didn't slip out for a smoke and Hann didn't get up to dance leaving it there for a few minutes?"

"To my certain knowledge, no. For a start off, I never went to the bar with her boyfriend. I don't like the fellow, so I left him to buy his own drinks."

Joe shook his head. "I'm glad I'm not dating your daughter. You don't go out of your way to make a guy feel welcome, do you?"

"Man's a barefaced fortune hunter," Prudhoe declared. "If I had my way I'd…"

"Let's not get into that," Joe cut him off. He chewed his lip.

"At some time between you buying this necklace for your daughter and presenting it to her this evening, someone has got to this parcel, and either exchanged it or removed the contents. Where did you keep it between the date you bought it and tonight?"

"In the safe at my home, and before you ask, no one but me knows the combination and I change it monthly."

Joe darted a quick glance at him, then concentrated on rolling another cigarette. "You solvent, Prudhoe?"

The effect was, as he anticipated, explosive. "WHAT? Are you suggesting –"

"I said we need to examine all possibilities," Joe interrupted tucking his cigarette into his shirt and putting the tobacco away.

Still fuming, Prudhoe demanded, "Have you ever heard of the Chiltern Hundreds?"

"Yes I have," Joe replied, and for the benefit of Yvonne and Geoff explained, "It's a nominal office under the Chancellor of the Exchequer and it's the only way an MP can resign his seat in the House of Commons. Once appointed to the Chiltern Hundreds, the MP can no longer hold his seat." He rounded on Prudhoe again. "I also know that once he's declared bankrupt, an MP has only six months to discharge his debts or he's compelled to resign."

Prudhoe smiled viciously. "And there I was thinking you were just an ignorant peasant. Well, forget it, Murray. I am not bankrupt. Nowhere near. The fifteen thousand I paid for this necklace is pocket money. Right?"

Joe shrugged. "As you wish." He fished into his pocket, ensuring he had his cigarette lighter with him. "It seems that what we have here is an impossible crime. A package put into the safe, not touched from the day it was purchased until it was opened by Hannah Prudhoe and yet the contents have disappeared."

"Unless one of these two touched it," Prudhoe said, his pointing finger wagging between Yvonne and Geoff.

"Or unless you removed it before you left it with us," Yvonne retorted.

"Now look here –"

"I'll not sit back and let you accuse me or my staff –"

"You'll have more than a mangled hand to contend with before I'm –"

"Try it, you loudmouthed –"

"All right, all right," Joe interrupted. "There's nothing to be gained by getting at each other's throats. Prudhoe, if I stole this necklace, how much would I get for it on the black market?"

Still simmering, the MP considered the question. "My guess would be no more than ten thousand. It's quite distinctive, so it would be difficult to sell on. If you were looking at a professional dealer in stolen goods…"

"A fence," Joe interpreted.

"A fence," Prudhoe agreed, "you'd be lucky to get two thousand for it."

"I don't see Yvonne, or Geoff, risking their careers for the sake of two thousand pounds," Joe declared, "and by the same token, you're no fool. I can't see you risking your reputation and career for a lousy ten grand, or even fifteen if you were looking to make a false insurance claim, so I don't think either of you had anything to do with its disappearance." He eyed them all individually. "But I can't rule any of you out completely."

A moment's grudging silence fell. The three occupants eyed each other up.

"So what's your theory?" Prudhoe asked.

"I don't have one," Joe confessed. "It seems to me we're not looking for a thief, but a magician."

Chapter Six

"You'd better have this right, Murray," Edgar warned. "If the thief has already got away with this –"

"You'll be able to claim on your insurance," Joe interrupted.

Almost half an hour had passed since they left Yvonne's office, and the crowd in the bar had thinned a little as a crowd of guests gathered in Reception for the ghost walk.

Joe waved at the room. "You see these people, Prudhoe. They're mostly my people. I know them. They're honest and hard working, and I'll swear there isn't a thief amongst them, unlike you and your friends, the bloodsucking leeches of Westminster. We're in the majority in this hotel tonight, so I know the only people likely to have stolen your necklace are from the staff or your crowd."

"Do you ever wonder why I don't like people like you?" Prudhoe demanded, a murderous gleam in his eye.

"Do you ever stop to wonder why people don't like you?"

"No, because I don't care."

"Then why would you expect me to give a hoot about you?" Joe demanded. "Now, you know what you're doing while I'm on the ghost walk?"

"Keeping an eye on Callum bloody McGuire."

"Correct. Use your head, Prudhoe. If it's Callum and he makes a move, don't get tempted to stop him."

The MP snorted. "What? Let him walk away with my daughter's birthday present. Not bloody likely."

Joe shook his head sadly. "It's all bluff with you, isn't it? He's twenty years younger than you, five stones lighter and built like a concrete khasi. He'll tear you to pieces, you idiot. If he's gonna run for it, let him go. He won't get far."

"What about the blonde with the hand, and her boyfriend?" Prudhoe demanded.

"I've got them covered," Joe reported, "but they won't know the difference unless they try to leg it."

Having dealt with the Honourable Gentleman, Joe made his way out to Reception and pushed through the small crowd gathering for the ghost walk. As he did so, he pressed his mobile to his ear to make it appear that he was in the middle of a call. When he made the counter, he closed it again and tucked it into his shirt pocket. Approaching Reception, he said to Yvonne, "I've called the cops in York. They'll have someone here within half an hour. You know what you're doing?"

She nodded towards the CCTV monitor hidden behind the counter. "Keeping an eye open for anyone who may suddenly decide to leave or anyone hanging around their own, or someone else's, car."

"And Geoff's at the door. No heroics," Joe ordered. "If they try to leave, let 'em. We only need the car details. The police will do everything else."

Again Yvonne agreed. "May I ask, Mr Murray, who's going to keep an eye on the Prudhoes?"

"I have that covered. Deidre and her daughter are going on the ghost walk, and I'll be with them. Edgar and the boyfriend, Callum, will be in the bar, and I have one or two of my people watching them."

"Good," Yvonne said. "I don't trust that man, or any of his family."

Agreeing with her, and taking her candid opinion with him, Joe stepped away from Reception, wriggled his way through the crowd gathered for the ghost walk, and joined Sheila and Brenda near the lifts.

While kicking their heels waiting for Linda Ellis, Sheila

asked, "What do you really think, Joe?"

Joe glanced furtively around to ensure no one was listening. There were about twenty people waiting for Linda Ellis, most of them STAC members. Yvonne stood at the counter about ten feet from them, Geoff was at the main entrance, ostensibly taking the night air. Deidre and Hannah Prudhoe were at the front of the crowd, the mother weaving slightly as if she were half drunk, while Edgar, he knew, was back in the bar with Callum, and Joe had asked George Robson, who was not attending the ghost walk, to keep an eye on them.

"I think at least one of them is lying," he said, keeping his voice down. "Judging from the setup, it would need more than any conjuror to get that package out of the safe, so either the necklace was never in the box, in which case it means that Prudhoe is pulling some kind of scam, or Yvonne Naylor and Geoff Vallance are working together and ripped Prudhoe off."

"So why all the palaver about keeping an eye on the main door?" Brenda asked.

"A ruse," Joe admitted. He checked his watch. "I've just spoken to Yvonne and she believes I've called the cops."

"But you haven't?" Sheila asked.

He grinned. "Not yet. I want to know who it is before I call the law. I told Prudhoe about five minutes ago that I was stepping outside to call the law because I couldn't hear properly in the bar."

Brenda frowned. "Great, so everyone believes PC Plod is on the way, even though he isn't. Where will that get you?"

"I'm hoping that the thought of the law turning up will panic the real culprit into some kind of action. See, what will happen if the police really do show? They'll speak to Yvonne, who will point them at me, because I carried out a preliminary inquiry. I'll tell them my suspicions, and the first thing the cops will do is search Yvonne, Geoff, and the Prudhoes. That thought should be enough to panic the real villain into hiding the necklace somewhere where a search won't turn it up."

"Where?" Brenda demanded.

"I don't know, do I?" Joe retorted. "But I'm hoping their actions will give us a clue."

Brenda considered this for a moment and then pointed out, "You have George watching the Prudhoes in the bar, you have us watching the mother and daughter on the ghost walk. So who's watching the manageress and her toy boy?" She pointed surreptitiously at Yvonne and Geoff as she named them.

Joe smiled again. "Keep watching and you'll find out."

Linda eased her way through the crowd to the front, standing just inside the main entrance, close to Geoff.

"Your attention ladies and gentlemen, please." She paused to let silence fall across the crowd. "Thank you. We're going to make our way across to the Old Inn. Now it's still raining and very blustery. Not good weather for umbrellas but perfect for hoodies. Once we get into the Old Inn, I'll give you the full story of Jack Palmer's ghost and then we'll hold a little vigil to see if we can contact his spirit. So if we're all ready?"

The crowd began to mill towards the exit. Without warning, Sylvia Goodson moaned and staggered slightly.

Les Tanner took her arm and led her to a seat. Joe, Sheila, Brenda and several others gathered round her.

"It's nothing," Sylvia said. "Honestly. Diabetes. I'll – I'll be all right in a moment."

Linda fought her way back through the crowd. "Is everything all right?"

"It's nothing," Sylvia assured her. "Just… you know. My blood sugar's a little erratic."

"You take these people on ahead," Tanner said to Linda. "I'll stay here with Sylvia."

Disappointment flashed across Linda's features to be replaced by a patronising smile. It happened so quickly that Joe thought he'd imagined it.

"Nonsense, Les," Sylvia insisted. "You go with them. I'll wait here. I was never bothered for ghost hunting anyway, but I know you were looking forward to it."

"But Sylvia…"

She cut Tanner off. "Les, I'll be all right here. The hotel staff will keep an eye on me, won't you?" She smiled at Yvonne and Geoff.

"Of course," Yvonne said. "Are you sure you don't need a doctor or something?"

"Dear me, no," Sylvia said. "I've had these do's before." She looked up into Tanner's concerned face. "Now, Les, stop fussing. Go and enjoy yourself with Joe and Sheila and Brenda."

After a few more moments of debate, the crowd finally filed out into the vicious night, turning left towards the back corner of The Palmer. Joe fished into his shirt pocket, took out a cigarette and lit it.

"Did you arrange that with Sylvia so she could keep an eye on Yvonne and Geoff?" Sheila asked out of the side of her mouth.

Blowing a thin cloud of smoke into the wind, Joe cackled softly. "You remember the September meeting in the Miner's Arms? There was a lot of arguing that day and I noticed Sylvia and the Cap'n disagreeing over something. It's not often you see that, is it?"

"Very rare. As a couple they never argue," Sheila agreed.

"Sylvia wasn't interested in ghost hunting. In fact, I think she'd have been happy with a day's shopping in York and a show, but Les *is* interested, especially with York having a history as a garrison town. I spoke to Sylvia in the bar, just now, before we all met in Reception, and mentioned I needed someone to keep an eye on the people at the front entrance. When I put it to them, Sylvia was all in favour. It was the perfect solution for us all. Sylvia misses the ghost walk and I get my spy. I thought she and Les played their parts perfectly, didn't you?"

"Les was in on it?" Brenda asked.

"How could I cut him out of it?" Joe asked. "You know what a pain in the backside he can be. Anyway, who better to keep an eye on the management than an old biddy suddenly taken ill with a diabetic hit?" He tapped the side of his nose. "There's always an advantage from having other people thinking you're an old duffer."

The wind buffeted them across the open expanse of car park at the back of the building. Joe took in the scene around him. No vehicles here, except for a Ford Transit van parked near the rear bar entrance. He guessed it would belong to Linda Ellis and her partner. It was the ideal place to park so they could transport their equipment into the hotel without cutting through Reception.

"You do know they turn the lights out for a minute, Joe," Sheila said.

He nodded and, cupping his hands against the wind, lit his cigarette again. "It doesn't matter. If our thief is going to run for it, he'll be missing when the lights go on again, won't he?"

"Suppose he tries to hide the necklace in the dark?" Brenda asked.

"Then the cops will find it when they get here and search the place, won't they?" He drew on the cigarette, got no response from it, and paused to re-light it. "The ghost walk is the only chance the culprit has, and we have all the angles covered."

Ahead of them, Linda reached the door to the Old Inn, and holding it open for her charges, ushered them in. Joe held back, to finish his cigarette, and while he struggled to draw from it, he assessed the front view of the Old Inn.

The upper front was mock-Tudor, done in traditional white with black beams zigzagging across it. The lower front was dark, apparently constructed of timber, but Joe had the feeling that if he examined it closely, he would find it was brick with wood cladding on the outside. The windows were small, square framed, small lights, many of them 'bulls-eye' panes. Jack o'lanterns hung either side of the door, swaying in the wind, but the light from them did not flicker. Store-bought, Joe guessed; plastic pumpkins employing low-wattage electric bulbs. This place had about as much history as the Lazy Luncheonette; less if he considered that the Sanford Main Colliery and nearby foundry had been targets of the Luftwaffe during World War Two.

"This place is about chasing the ghost of a profit," he muttered

"Sorry, Mr Murray. I didn't catch that."

He found Linda waiting for him to follow the others into the building. "Nothing," he said. "Talking to myself." He tried to take a final drag of his cigarette. To his disgust it had gone out again. He threw it in a bin and then gestured along the front of the building to the stables, where a door hung half open, swaying erratically in the wind. "What's in there?"

"Those are the stables," Linda explained. "We don't go in there. The Palmer uses it as a sort of junk house, where they throw old and broken furniture."

"A glory hole, huh?"

It certainly looked the part from Joe's point of view. The building appeared as if it had been tagged onto the Old Inn as an afterthought. Constructed of timber, the pitched roof, its angle quite shallow, was covered with felt, not slate or shingle, and at odd places in the wall, planks had been nailed into place to plug holes.

He sensed Linda getting impatient and moved into the inn.

The interior was laid out as an old pub, but behind the ramshackle bar, there were no drinks, only glasses and empty bottles, and to the left hand end, from Joe's point of view, a large, closed cupboard.

Looking further around, he noticed immediately that the floor was clear of dust. The Palmer, eager to maintain a front, obviously sent cleaners in at least on the day preceding the monthly ghost walk. The tables and chairs, many of them simple, three-legged stools, had all been pushed to one end of the room, leaving a large, clear space in the centre, where the crowd congregated. In the far right corner, a flight of rickety wooden steps led to the upper floor. Joe did not like the look of them, and he hoped they were not going to visit the top floor. The stairs did not look solid enough to support one person, never mind two dozen.

In the left corner, he spotted an open door, and through it, only just visible in the poor lighting, he could make out a heap of what looked like old wood. It took a moment to register as a broken dresser, and the wood panel beyond it as a stall in the stables. Access to the stables from here, the doors beyond open to the car park? If the thief were going to make a run for it, that would be the route.

He made a note of those nearest the stable exit. Hannah Prudhoe and a couple of STAC members, one of whom was Les Tanner. Joe himself, stood between Sheila, on his left, and Brenda, with Deidre Prudhoe, still swaying as if she were out in the strong winds, to Sheila's left. To Brenda's right were Alec and Julia Staines. Closing the door behind her, Linda insinuated herself into the circle to the Staines' right, nudging Alec over a little. She seemed quite determined to stand there. Joe glanced back at the door and, beyond its hinges, hidden when the door was open, he could see a bank of light switches, over which hung a shiny disc affair with wires leading to the floor and behind a stool. Looking closely he could make out a large battery also behind the stool. Joe followed the wires up from the disc and cross the ceiling and saw that the thin lights illuminating this shambolic room were not the main ones, but a separate set which had been rigged up as a temporary measure.

He silently congratulated Linda and whoever she was working with. They had the set up just about perfect. He couldn't see where the 'ghost' was hiding, but the cupboard at the end of the bar had a telltale hole drilled into it. About three-quarters of an inch in diameter, it was set somewhere near eye-level. Ideal for aiming an infrared remote to cut off the lights.

He also congratulated himself. He may be in his mid-fifties, but his lightning mind was as sharp now as it had been when he was a lad.

Linda began to speak and everyone, Joe included, honed their attention upon her.

"Welcome, ladies and gentlemen, to the Old Inn. Although the present building was erected sometime during the nineteenth century, older buildings have stood on this spot for over 600 years, but it was in the eighteenth century that the Old Inn at Elvington became notorious. On the night of October 30th 1750, highwayman, Jack Palmer, returned to this place, his favourite haunt, where the maid, Sarah Strensall, served him with a meal and afterwards helped him attend his horse. It's said that while they were in the stables, Jack seduced Sarah for the first time. The landlord, so enraged that a villain could seduce a maid whom he himself coveted, had already warned the constable that Palmer would come, and while highwayman and maid lay entwined in each other's arms in the stables, the local Justices arrived with militiamen and tried to arrest him. A fight followed during which shots were fired. In the darkness, Sarah Strensall lay dead and Jack Palmer was missing. It's said he lay hidden in a priest's hole here in the inn, where he was found, and dragged crying his innocence to York prison. Tried and sentenced to death by hanging, as he was carried to the gallows at Knavesmire, near to where York Racecourse now stands, he cursed the Old Inn, swearing that he would haunt its walls for eternity."

Linda lowered her voice to a stage hush.

"Ever since, there have been reports of ghostly manifestations here in the Old Inn. Guests would be disturbed during the hours of darkness, personal possessions would be stolen from them, only to turn up in the stables later in the night. At length the disturbances became so bad that the village people burned the Old Inn to the ground. It was rebuilt as it is now in 1815… but the hauntings continued until things reached the stage where no one would stay here. The Old Inn has remained uninhabited since 1830, and yet still the disturbances happen and many is The Palmer Hotel guest who has strayed into the Old Inn and found his possessions stolen, only to have them returned later in the night. It's said that it's the ghost of Jack Palmer who, even in death, cannot break his old habits of stealing."

Linda took her voice even lower until it was not much above a whisper.

"As we look around this Old Inn, guard your possessions well and say a silent prayer for the soul of Jack Palmer that he may leave you as he finds you."

"What do you say to those who consider this tale so much twaddle?" Sheila asked.

"I've been here many a time, Mrs Riley, and I've felt the presence of some... *something*. Not quite evil, but mischievous."

"So you don't accept that this ghostly scenario was dreamt up by the group who own The Palmer simply to increase trade?"

Joe gave credit to Sheila for her persistence. She'd spent most of her working life in a school and even though she had never been a teacher, she nevertheless valued good education, which involved history as it was, not as some large corporation would have the public believe it was.

Linda returned a wan smile. "I can't comment on that, Mrs Riley. I wasn't even born in the seventies." Their guide opened up her attention to the group. "Now, if we're all quiet, if we all tune our minds to the building, maybe one or two of us, those sensitive enough to pick up the vibrations, may get to experience Jack Palmer."

Silence fell over the group. They looked around the place, they looked up at the ceiling, they looked down at the floor. Alec Staines suppressed a nervous snigger when his wife, Julia, elbowed him.

"Jack," Linda said "Are you with us, Jack?"

Joe glanced at her. As she spoke, she opened her clenched fist, showing four fingers. He frowned. Four fingers? What did that mean?

"Give us a sign that you're here, Jack," Linda asked.

From somewhere above and in the distance came a thud. Joe felt Sheila jump. Many of the others were startled by it, too, but what intrigued him most was Linda. As the sound occurred, she open her fist, showing four fingers and her thumb, closed it again and then opened it with only one finger showing. Six, this time. First four, now six. What did it mean?

"Is that you, Jack? Are you here? Give us a sign, Jack."

Again there was a distant thump. The circle of people appeared nervous. He noticed Julia Staines taking hold of her husband's hand and Les Tanner coughed to hide his own worries. This time Linda opened and closed her fist twice, both times showing all five digits, then opened it a third time, showing only two fingers.

Four, six and now twelve.

Joe had to silently congratulate the girl. He didn't know who she was signalling to, he didn't know what the signals meant, but she made them so quickly and at such a stage of proceedings that only someone with Joe's acute powers of observation would notice them.

***

In the cupboard, where he stood stock still and completely silent, Rick took in Linda's signals and committed them to memory. Numbers four, six and twelve.

His spy hole was not large enough to give him all round vision of the circle, so he could not see who they were. He could make out number four; the little guy wearing the pale green fisherman's vest over his woolly jumper. According to Linda, there was a Zippo lighter in the right hand pocket.

Rick could also see number six, the politician's wife, but he could not see far enough round the circle to identify number twelve. He must be the Duke of Wellington as Linda had identified him in the bar. Silver pen in the top pocket, she had said.

Taking a deep breath to charge his muscles with oxygen, he pulled his night vision lens into place, switched it on, and aimed his infrared remote.

***

When the lights went out, the room was plunged into total darkness. Not even the faint lights from The Palmer or the jack o'lanterns could penetrate it.

"Stay calm, ladies and gentlemen," Linda urged as some woman let out a sharp cry.

Joe reached to his pocket for his cigarette lighter. Alec Staines beat him to it, but as Alec lit the room briefly, a dark shape moving quickly round the perimeter of the circle, snuffed it out. Then something nudged Brenda. She screamed and fell into Joe. He felt her jostle him, almost knocking him from his feet. He forgot about his cigarette lighter, and put out his hand to steady her. It took hold of something a lot softer than her arm and Joe had momentary visions, enhanced by the total blackness, of why Brenda was so appealing to men.

Sheila moved as Joe swayed into her, and the knock-on effect forced Deidre Prudhoe to move inwards from the edge of the circle. Deidre screamed and the person the other side of her – Joe had an idea it was one of his members but he couldn't think who – let out a gasp. A second later, it was Hannah Prudhoe crying out, "Mum!" followed quickly by Les Tanner, gasping, "What the ruddy hell…"

"Stay calm and remain still, ladies and gentlemen," Linda urged. "Jack is amongst us. He won't stay long. He never does. Soon he will return to the spirit realm and then grant us light to see by."

Reminded of the darkness, Joe reached into his pocket again, searching for his Zippo, and was irritated when he could not find it.

"You okay, Brenda?" he asked.

"Not as much as you should be after giving me such a good grope."

Joe did not trust himself to say anything, but ferreted in his left pocket and still could not find his lighter. "Where the hell is it?"

The lights came on.

"Thank you, Jack," said Linda, poker-faced.

The small crowd gave her a smattering of applause.

"This is serious, ladies and gentlemen," she responded. "Jack has visited you. I would urge you to check your pockets and see if anything is missing."

Everyone began to fumble in their pockets.

"Would you like me to search you, Joe?" Brenda asked seductively.

"I can manage," he replied.

"You managed my left bubble," she told him.

Joe continued to root through his pockets. "It was accidental. I was trying to hold you up."

"Pray God that I should be mugged every day like that," Brenda breathed.

On the other side of Joe, Sheila tittered. "I can see you two ending up as lovers."

"It'll be a cold day in Grimsby before that happens," Joe told her.

"Grimsby?" Sheila asked. "You mean hell."

"Hell, Grimsby. There's not much difference."

"Good lord," said Les Tanner. "Me pen's gone."

"Yeah. And my Zippo lighter," Joe grumbled.

The crowd muttered between themselves, most of it relief after the few scary minutes of darkness, now translated into admiration for Linda and the performance she and her unseen partner had put on.

"Any items taken usually turn up in the bar," Linda assured them. "And now ladies and gentlemen, I think we've tempted

Jack enough for one night, so if we make our way back over to the bar, the rest of the evening's entertainment can carry on."

The crowd began to break up. As it did so, Joe looked around the circle again, and the obvious dawned on him. He was fourth from the left of Linda; as he counted quickly round, he made Deidre as the sixth and Les Tanner as number 12. Strange then, that Deidre had not said anything about losing personal items.

"Careful as we step outside, please" Linda urged them. "It's still raining and blowing a gale, but there's plenty more fun to come over in the bar."

"That's all very well for you," Joe said, "but what do I do for a smoke in the meantime?"

Brenda linked her arm in his. "Stick with me, baby. I'll make the both of us smoke."

Chapter Seven

Joe finally managed to disentangle himself from Brenda when they got back to the entrance, where he and Alec Staines elected to stay under the shelter of the portico for a smoke.

Taking a light from Alec, Joe commented on Deidre's silence after the ghost show. When Alec asked why she should comment, Joe related his deductions and Alec applauded.

"Clever piece of observation, that, Joe, though I'm not surprised, knowing you." Alec blew out a cloud of smoke. "As for her, well, she's so blathered, she wouldn't know if she was on this earth or fuller's earth."

"Drunk?" Joe was surprised. "She was sober enough when I spoke to her earlier."

"You haven't seen how she puts the voddie away? It's like giving a thirsty dog a dish of water one thimbleful at a time."

Joe slotted the information into the correct compartments of his mind, as an explanation for the way she was swaying when they left for the Old Inn and while they were in there. In his view it also eliminated her from possible collusion with her husband on the missing necklace. If she was a routine drunkard, Prudhoe would know, and while he would probably cover up for her (a man in his position could hardly let it become known that his wife had an alcohol problem) he would not trust her to assist him with anything so finely balanced as a potential insurance fraud.

"But that doesn't eliminate Prudhoe himself," Sheila pointed out when she and Joe travelled up to the third floor together in the lift.

"No. But I still think that if he's trying to pull a fast one with his insurers, he's taking an awful risk. If anyone rumbles it, he's in serious trouble."

"And if anyone can rumble it, you can, Joe."

The lift doors opened and they stepped out.

"Talking of rumbling," Sheila asked as they walked along to their respective rooms, "what's this new found tactile thing with Brenda?"

"Nothing," Joe said, and checked to see if she was joking. Her face remained serious, and he pleaded. "It was an accident, Sheila. I swear it. Someone nudged her, she screamed and fell into me. I thought she was falling, so I put my arm sort of under her shoulder to stop her and I got hold of her..." he trailed off, his eyes willing her to believe him.

Sheila smiled. "It's all right, Joe. We're all adults. I'll change my shoes and see you down in the bar."

Joe entered his room, threw off his damp gilet, and his jumper, which he hung over the radiator to dry, then put on a fresh one before putting the damp gilet over it again.

"Me and Brenda?" he snorted at his reflection. "A roll on the rug, maybe, but that'll be the bloody day when she becomes Mrs Murray mark two."

***

Ten minutes later, in the bar, Sheila and Brenda were having a similar conversation, and Brenda was forced to laugh when Sheila told her of Joe's performance outside his room.

"I'm sure it was accidental," Brenda said, "but he did get a good handful."

Sheila eyed Brenda's larger bosom with a touch of envy. "You've always had a couple of handfuls for any man," she said. "So you're not thinking of getting serious with Joe?"

Brenda laughed again and downed a large swallow of

Campari. "Good grief, no. I mean, I think Joe is a wonderful man, but don't you dare tell him that."

"Cross my heart," Sheila promised.

"And I'll cross my legs." Brenda giggled again. "I think Joe is a smashing bloke and I might be tempted to a roll in the hay with him, but I'd never let it get serious. I don't want another husband, for a start off, and if I did, he'd have to be someone less dedicated to his work and hoarding money than Joe." Brenda's brow knitted quizzically. "You're not thinking of…"

Sheila shook her head. "No, I'm not. Mostly for the same reasons as you. I'm not interested in marrying again. Joe has the potential to be a good husband, but like the road to hell, such a relationship would be paved with good intentions and major fights. I just wanted to make sure I wasn't in your way. We've been friends for a long time, and I wouldn't want to spoil that."

"Me neither. Neither would the maestro." Brenda nodded to the entrance where Joe had just walked in. "Talking of the man, here he is."

***

Still preoccupied, Joe had called first at Reception where both Yvonne and Geoff had nothing to report.

"No one made a dash for it, Mr Murray," Yvonne assured him, "and we haven't seen any vehicles rushing out of the car park."

Puzzled, Joe thanked them, and entered the bar. Looking around, he saw Brenda and Sheila in conversation on a table by the back wall, but disregarded them, looking around for Sylvia. He didn't see her, but Les Tanner's military get up was impossible to miss. Joe weaved his way through the tables and sat with them for a minute or two.

"Neither of them left the building, Joe," Sylvia reported. "If they're your thieves, they're playing it very cool."

Again Joe frowned. Thanking Sylvia, he called at the bar,

collected drinks, and made for his two companions. He had not gone five paces, when Prudhoe waylaid him.

"Well?"

"Nothing," Joe said. "Not one damned movement out of place. It's crazy. Whoever he is, he had the perfect opportunity, but didn't take it."

"Right," said the MP. "That's it. I'm calling the cops."

"No need," Joe lied. "I already called them. Before we went on the ghost walk. They should be here soon."

"Oh." Prudhoe appeared slightly taken aback. He glanced at his watch. "In that case, I'll wait for them, but if anyone tries to leave –"

"No one will leave," Joe cut in. "If they try, we'll have 'em. Now, if you'll excuse me."

Joe continued his journey across the lounge, and was joined by George Robson as he reached the table.

"Well, as master plans go, Joe, that was about as good as England's for the last World Cup," George said. "Prudhoe and the boyfriend never moved and never spoke to one another. According to Sylvia, Yvonne never left Reception and the other nurk, Geoff is he called, stood shivering in the rain at the front entrance."

"And as if that's not enough, the ghost of Jack Palmer nicked his lighter," Brenda laughed.

Sheila was not laughing. Her face was set into a stern mask of disapproval. "You're going to look a complete idiot, Joe, when the police, allegedly on their way, don't show up."

"And you think I don't know that?" Joe's frown deepened. "Why didn't they go for it?" he muttered. "It has to be one of them, I gave them the perfect opportunity to make their move and they didn't. Why?"

"Perhaps it wasn't one of them," Brenda suggested. "Maybe there really was a sneak thief who broke into the office and raided the safe."

"How? Huh?" Joe demanded. "How did he get in there? The

84

office has not been left empty all day."

"Pull the other one," Brenda said. "Let me draw you a picture. Sonny Jim, big Geoff, fancies Yvonne. You only have to look at him to know that. I think that manky hand is putting him off. Yvonne has issues. The same hand. Geoff needs to steel himself to ask for her knickers in bed, and if she wants to encourage him, she'll try to put it out of mind and sight. Now let's say Geoff has invited her home for coffee and, er, embellishments…"

Sheila laughed. "That's a new word for it."

"I'm trying to be polite," Brenda said, haughtily. "I don't want to embarrass Joe and George."

George roared with laughter but before he could speak Joe got in.

"Just get on with it," he ordered Brenda.

"So there's Yvonne looking forward to a tasty cup of coffee with Geoff as dessert. She's getting a bit excited. Geoff isn't about, but she needs to tart herself up a bit, so she slopes off to the little girls' room. While she's gone, the office door may be locked, but the thief sees his opportunity, gets in – maybe he's a member of staff and he has a key – and she's left the keys for the safe on the desk. Perfect. He has a replacement parcel ready. He nicks the original, sticks the label on his replacement and clears off. The perfect crime."

Joe nodded. "Can't fault it," he said. "And this opportunist thief not only has a replacement parcel ready, but inside it an absolutely identical presentation box for the necklace."

Brenda's cheeks and ears coloured and her face fell. "Oh. I never thought of that."

"Remember Occam's Razor?" Sheila said. "Filey, during the summer? One must not multiply logical entities without underlying evidence."

George frowned. "I'm a wet shaver, myself."

"You're an idiot," Sheila declared. "And Brenda cracked that same gag in Filey."

Puzzled, George asked, "What gag? Can we stop talking about razors and try plain English?"

Sheila tutted again. "What it boils down to, George, is that the simplest explanation is the most logical. The only people who could have stolen that necklace are those who had easiest access to it. And on the face of it, Joe is right. It must be either Yvonne and Geoff working in league, or the Prudhoes. But Joe's plan hasn't got us any further forward. In fact, it could get him into trouble. Especially when Prudhoe learns the police are not coming, and calls them himself."

"And when they do get here, the cops won't wanna look for my lighter."

***

Taking a last tour round the Old Inn, Rick checked his haul. Just as Linda had said. Nothing spectacular, but enough to give the audience a laugh; a Zippo lighter from Darth Vader's gilet, a silver-plated Schaeffer pen from the top pocket of Wellington's tunic, and a plastic bag from Deidre Prudhoe's pocket, which he checked to ensure the contents were all right.

The evening's entertainment was almost ready to move into its final phase. There were times when they had to be careful about returning items. It did not happen often, but he'd once lifted a man's wallet containing, not money but photographs of his wife or girlfriend in what could be termed alluring poses. Alluring? That was putting it mildly. Outright indecent, they were. For obvious reasons, he could not place the wallet for its owner to 'find' when Linda guided him. Instead, he handed it over discreetly as he returned to the bar.

Climbing the ladder to take down his temporary lights, he thought that one day, when he was in his dotage, perhaps he would write a book on the things he had come across; objects that told him much more about people and personalities than anyone could learn by talking to them.

"Listen, Brenda, while Sheila's at the bar, I wanted to talk to you about what happened in the Old Inn."

Brenda smiled broadly at Joe. "Just forget about it. I know it was accidental."

"No, it's not that," Joe said. "It's the way you were going on afterwards, and I know you were mainly joking, but I need to clear the air."

Brenda's face became more serious. "That sounds ominous."

"Not really, but I need to say what I need to say and I'm trying to find a way of doing it tactfully, so I don't hurt your feelings or anything."

She sighed. "I've known you since we were kids, Joe, and I've never known you worry about hurting anyone's feelings. I've never known you to be diplomatic, either. You're usually about as tactful as a thirty-ton truck. Just say it."

"Well, see, I think you and Sheila are probably the best friends I've ever had. No. Not probably. Definitely. But I was married once. I didn't like it and there's no way I'll ever make the same mistake again. I'm not interested in either of you, er, that way."

Brenda's face split into her broadest grin. "I think we already know that, Joe. In fact, we were talking about it while you were upstairs getting changed."

"You were?"

"Hmm," Brenda nodded. "I think, and Sheila does too, that you'd make a wonderful provider, but a lousy husband."

Taking out his tobacco and rolling a cigarette, Joe scowled. "Thanks for nothing."

"No, seriously, Joe. You're too wrapped up in your work, your puzzles and the club, to be a proper husband. You're also a serial tightwad, as you frequently admit. Like I said, you'd be a good provider. Any woman trapping you into wedlock would want for nothing. But there'd be some awful rows."

Sheila returned with the drinks and Joe lapsed into his thoughts. Hadn't someone said something similar earlier?

***

With the noise of Sammy Davis Jnr belting out a souped-up version of *That Old Black Magic,* Linda barely heard her mobile ring. She looked around at those closest to her. Could they hear what she was saying?

Taking it from her pocket, she opened it and put it to her ear. "Rick? What? I can't hear you…" She raised her voice and heads turned her way. "I said, I can't hear… Just get over here and tell me then. These people will be getting anxious about their property."

***

With the dance floor so crowded, Joe found it difficult to keep his eye on the Prudhoes' table. Brenda and Sheila were taking turns to go to the bar entrance and watch Yvonne and Geoff, and he had George Robson stationed the other side of the room, also supposedly keeping an eye on the Prudhoe family, but he knew George. It didn't take much more than a fluttering eyelash or a flash of leg to distract him.

"Give it up, Joe," Sheila suggested. "The ghost walk was over almost half an hour ago. Whatever you thought they were going to do, they didn't, and it won't be long before they start asking where the police are."

He took out his mobile phone. "Maybe you're right. I'd better go to the door and call them out for real, huh?"

"It would make sense. It may come down to a search of everyone and their rooms, but at least they'll get to the bottom of it."

A familiar head of dark hair bobbed its way round the dance

floor, heading for the exit. Joe stood up and looked over at the Prudhoes' table. It was empty. He checked the dance floor and then the bar. He could see none of them.

Joe's pulse increased. "What were you saying?" he demanded.

As Edgar left the bar, he followed. Pausing at the entrance, he watched as the MP turned left out into the night, towards the Old Inn. Joe hurried out into Reception. No sign of either Yvonne or Geoff, and the office door was closed. He rang the bell and waited a moment. No answer.

"Fine stake-out detectives you two would make," he grumbled and hurried out into the night. No sign of Prudhoe, either, but the Bentley was still there.

He hurried along the side of the hotel to the corner, and stared across the rear car park to the Old Inn. His face split into a broad grin. The door was closed, but through the tiny, bulls-eye panes, he could make out light inside. Nice try, Prudhoe, he thought, but not fast enough to catch out Joe Murray.

Soaking wet, his gilet, recently dried out, now drenched again, Joe fairly sprinted across the open tarmac and pressed his ear to the wooden door of the Old Inn. He could hear nothing. Not a sound. He checked the windows. The light he had seen flickering earlier was gone, too, and the place was in total darkness. His earlier visit had told him where to find the light switch, so all he had to do was…

Quick as a flash, he threw the door open and rushed in. Reaching up, fumbling in the dark, he snapped on the lights. "Right, Prudhoe, I've… "

He trailed off and stared at the floor.

Edgar Prudhoe lay where he had fallen, a deep weal in the back of his head. Alongside him lay a long, metal bar, the handle of a bottle jack if Joe was not mistaken.

He hurried over, crouched, and pressed a reluctant hand to Prudhoe's neck.

Dead.

Standing upright, Joe immediately worried for his own

safety. If the killer were still here, he could be in danger, too. Then he looked down at the metal bar, and relaxed a little.

But not much.

Behind the bar, the cupboard, where he guessed Rick Hart had hidden during the ghost walk, was wide open. The temporary lights had been taken down, and now lay in a bundle on one of the tables, above the heavy duty battery which powered them. The crocodile clips which attached the sensor to the battery had been disconnected, and they, too, lay on the table. A glance at the far corner revealed the exit to the stables open. Joe cursed himself. He had not noticed whether the exterior door to the stables, further along the Old Inn building, was open.

He hurried over, paused, and cautiously looked into the stables. There were four stalls, all littered with old and broken furniture: chairs, bar tables, dining tables, bedside dressers from the rooms, cluttered the place, and inconsequentially, he wondered why the hotel did not take advantage of events like Guy Fawkes Night, just a few days away, to get rid of this junk.

The far door, leading back to the car park, was open, and Joe knew he was in no danger. Edgar Prudhoe's killer had gone, run off into the night.

Reluctantly, he trudged back into the Old Inn, dug into his shirt pocket, pulled out his mobile, and dialled his niece, Detective Sergeant Gemma Craddock. Once through to her, he secured the number for York CID and then rang them.

"Palmer Hotel, Elvington, near York," he said when he finally got through. "We have a dead body on our hands, and he's been murdered."

Chapter Eight

Preparing himself for the trudge back to the hotel, pure anger burning through his veins, Joe looked down on the lifeless form and it fuelled his anger even more. The York police had taken a little persuading, but his irritation had soon put that right, and now his fury settled on the dead man.

"I don't know what you were playing at, Prudhoe, but this isn't how it was supposed to turn out, is it?"

The noise of a diesel engine, roaring into life outside on the car park, brought Joe to his senses. Adrenaline surged through him. The killer!

With a curse, he rushed out of the Old Inn in time to see the dark blue Ford Transit, a cloud of blue/white smoke belching from its cold exhaust, turn the corner to run along the front of the hotel, making for the exit.

Joe dashed to the corner and as he arrived, the van braked and stopped alongside Linda Ellis, then the brake lights went out, and it roared away, turning left out of the hotel car park towards York. Linda ran after it, screaming at the night. "Rick."

For a moment Joe thought she was calling for her partner back in the hotel, but when she ran out into the road, he realised her partner was driving the van. Hadn't he guessed earlier that the van belonged to them?

"Linda," he shouted as she staggered to a halt and stared out along the main road. "Linda, you won't catch him. He's gone."

Head hanging, she turned and trudged back to the hotel. "What's got into him?" She looked up and her face was frantic with worry. "He's supposed to come back to the bar and give you your stuff back."

"Gimme the registration number of your van," Joe barked.

She frowned. "What? Look, my partner's just…"

"Don't argue," he growled taking out his mobile and redialling the police. "Just gimme the damn number." A few seconds later, he was through. "This is Joe Murray. I called about two or three minutes ago to report a murder at The Palmer Hotel, Elvington… Yes, yes. That's me. Now listen carefully: one of the suspects has just left the hotel in a hurry… I don't care what you think, you stupid mare, I'm telling you what's happ… All right, all right, I'm sorry. I shouldn't have said that. Now will you please listen? The suspect has just left The Palmer Hotel and he's heading for York in a dark blue Ford Transit van. Hold on, I'll give you the registration." He looked to Linda. "The number?"

Tears streaked her shocked, disbelieving face. "Rick? Murder? I don't –"

"Give me the bloody number," Joe snapped.

She stammered it out and Joe repeated it to the police.

"You should know me," he argued with the civilian receptionist on the phone. "If you have any doubts call Detective Sergeant Gemma Craddock in Sanford. She'll vouch for me. Now get someone onto that van and get your team down to The Palmer…" He paused to listen again, then spoke to Linda. "Where will Rick be headed? Your home?"

"It could be," she replied. "Or his parents, or some of his friends. I don't know. What –"

"Where's home?"

"I, er –"

"Listen to me," Joe ordered. "Every second that you dither gives him another few hundred yards on us. Now where the hell do you come from?"

"Bradford." She told him. "Wibsey in Bradford. His parents come from Idle. He could head for either end of the town."

Joe passed the information to the police and concluded, "If you've anything about you, you'll have heard of me. If not, like I said, talk to Detective Sergeant Craddock in Sanford, or better yet, get onto one of your own. Detective Sergeant Cummins. Terry Cummins knows me from his days in Sanford… What? Oh. He's Chief Inspector Cummins now, is he? Well, speak to him. He knows me."

Joe cut the connection, and then rang Sheila. After speaking briefly to her, he closed the phone, dropped it back into his shirt pocket, and looked into the eyes of Linda Ellis as if just realising that she was on the verge of breaking down. He gripped her gently by the elbow and led her back into the hotel.

"Come on. Let's get in out of this rain."

Geoff met him in the entrance. Sheila and Brenda hurried from the bar.

"Joe, whatever is going on?" Sheila asked.

"The weekend from hell," he replied. "Brenda, take Linda somewhere quiet, maybe Yvonne's office or the dining room, and get a large brandy down her. Try to keep her calm."

"You need to get out of those wet clothes, Linda," Geoff said. "I'll get a set of hotel issue for you. Not fashionable, but at least they'll be dry."

"Good thinking," Joe agreed. "Sheila, go into the bar, get the Prudhoe family together and bring them out here. And you'd better prepare them for some bad news."

Geoff's eyes opened. "Bad news?"

"Edgar Prudhoe is dead. He's laid out in the Old Inn."

Geoff seemed to stagger. Joe's companions looked him in the eye and he knew that they knew he was not fooling around. He would never joke over something so serious. Linda broke down, crying.

"I'd better get Yvonne down here, and we need to call the police," Geoff said and narrowed an angry stare on Joe. "They never turned up after you allegedly rung them."

"They're on their way now," Joe said while Brenda led Linda

to the dining room and Sheila hurried into the bar. "I called them the minute I discovered Prudhoe's body. Where is Yvonne, by the way?"

"On a break," Geoff replied. "We work long shifts, Mr Murray. She's gone to her room for a bit of shuteye. We're due off at midnight, but she hadn't had a break all day, so I suggested she take it now. What exactly has happened?"

Joe shrugged. "I don't know. Prudhoe was dead when I walked in. He'd been hit on the back of the head with a jack handle. Judging by the size of it, it may have come from Rick's van…"

He trailed off momentarily, his eyes glazing as he tripped his mind over the events. Something, he knew, was not right about that. Something he had just said did not ring true.

He became aware the others were waiting for him to speak. Clearing his throat, he said, "I rang the law and the next thing I knew, Rick's van was tearing out the gates with Linda running after it. It looks like Rick killed him and then decided to run for it."

Geoff's face was a picture of incredulity. "But why?"

"I can only imagine it has something to do with the missing necklace."

Joe shivered and suddenly became conscious of how wet he was, never mind Linda. "Look, I need to get upstairs and change out of these wet clothes, too. We'll know more when the cops get him. I gave them his registration."

***

Once back in his room, Joe threw off his wet clothing, grateful that he'd brought a change with him. He showered as a means of both warming up and wakening himself.

He was angry; more with himself than with anyone else. With hindsight, it was obvious that the killer must have been quite close when Joe entered the Old Inn. If he'd been thinking logically, he would have backed out of the place and probably caught the man... or woman.

But instead, he had reacted as most people would have done. Gone over to see what, if anything, he could do for Edgar Prudhoe, and the murderer – he assumed it was Rick, Linda's partner – had used those few moments to get away.

Towelling off, pulling on a dry shirt and a pair of denims, he knew that Sheila and Brenda would say he did the right thing. If he'd tried to tackle Rick, a much younger man, he, too, could have been struck by an iron bar and he, too, could have been on his way to hospital... or the mortuary. Even without the jack handle, Rick would have been too strong for him. It was the very reason he did not fully relax in the Old Inn.

The gilet was still damp. Joe removed it again and put it over the heaters. Digging into the pockets, he fished out a pack of cigarette papers and his disposable lighter. Both were soaked. The cigarette papers would be glued together by the time they dried out and he doubted that the lighter would ever work again. He threw both in the waste bin, opened his small suitcase, and took out a fresh pack of Rizla papers and a replacement, disposable lighter.

"Never let it be said that Joe Murray isn't prepared for every eventuality," he said to the empty room.

The murderer hadn't been prepared for his arrival; that was for sure. He'd panicked, dropped the weapon, and legged it.

Knowing that he would have to go back out into the night at some point, Joe picked up his coat ready to leave the room. He frowned. Something still troubled him, and it had to do with that murder weapon. What was it?

A full half hour passed before Joe returned to the bar to find Sheila and Brenda managing the disco. He could see no sign of Linda or the Prudhoes.

"They're in the manager's office with the police," Sheila reported, leaving Billy Fury to entertain the dancers with *Like*

I've Never Been Gone.

"No word on the runaway?" Joe asked picking up half of bitter and swallowing a mouthful.

"None," Sheila reported. "Seems like an open and shut case, Joe. He killed Prudhoe and then ran."

Joe nodded, but his eyes spelled doubt. "Isn't it always the way. It's only when you start to ask deeper questions that you realise it's not open and shut."

Listening in while studying the computer listing of tracks she could play for the dancers, Brenda asked, "Deeper questions such as?"

Joe shrugged. "Why did he run? It doesn't make a lot of sense. He's just brained Prudhoe with a jack handle. Technically, no one knew he was there, so why not just sneak back to his van, drop the handle in the back, then climb in the driver's seat and pretend to be asleep?"

"Panic?" Sheila suggested. "Perhaps he had an arranged meeting with Prudhoe, they argued, it got out of hand, and he didn't mean to kill him, but just landed out."

Joe shook his head. "Doesn't work. Listen, I was less than two minutes behind Prudhoe. That's not enough time for an argument to develop and get out of hand. Not to that degree anyway."

"All right then," Brenda argued, "he heard you coming and then panicked."

Again Joe disagreed. "Two things. If he dropped the jack handle and ran for it, I would have heard it hit the floor, and I didn't. That means he put the handle down before I even got to the door. Second, if he was that hyped up, he'd more than likely pick it up again and wait for me to come in so he could brain me with it."

"You're lucky he didn't," she said.

"That crossed my mind, too," Joe agreed. "The way it looks to me, this was pre-planned. The killer was waiting for Prudhoe, knowing he would be coming over there, and struck him with the intention of shuffling him off the mortal coil. So why run? Why drop the handle at all? Why not take it with him? You're right when you say he may have been panicked by my presence, but when I switched on the lights, there was no sign of him. He'd already snuck out the side door, through the stables, and legged it. If it was Rick wossname, the most sensible thing for him to do was drop the handle in his van, then come into the bar and plead total ignorance."

"So you're saying it wasn't the DJ?" Brenda asked.

"No, I'm simply saying his actions are not consistent, and it's not as open and shut as you may think." He took out his tobacco tin as Brenda switched from Billy Fury to the Swinging Blue Jeans. "How did the widow Prudhoe take it?"

"Shocked, naturally," Sheila replied. "But she's also very drunk and the news did nothing to sober her up. The daughter is thoroughly distraught, but the boyfriend is trying to console her."

Quickly rolling a cigarette, Joe fished in his pockets for his lighter. "Damn. It's still missing. According to Linda, her boyfriend has it. He was supposed to come to the bar and give us back the things he took during the ghost walk." He rooted through his gilet and came out with a cheap, disposable. "I'm going for a smoke and then I'll see if I can get a word with the investigating officer."

Picking up his topcoat and slipping it on, he left the podium, and cut a path through the dancing couples, into Reception where he rang the bell. A moment later, Geoff Vallance emerged from the office.

"You got the senior CID man in there?" Joe asked, and Geoff nodded. "Tell him I'm at the door having a smoke when he wants me."

Geoff agreed and Joe took himself to the front entrance where he lit a cigarette and gazed gloomily out on the appalling night.

The wind showed no signs of easing and the rain came down

in blustery sheets. His insides were in as much turmoil; the thrill of the (intellectual) chase, the proximity to a killing, compounded by the anger and futility of another human life lost. No matter how much Edgar Prudhoe warranted a lesson in manners or a good hiding, he did not deserve the brutality of such a violent death.

Joe puffed on his cigarette, his mind running over the rapid chain of events, reminding himself of the sequence. Human memory was fickle and frail. His never was. He had spent years training himself to observe, to remember. He knew precisely what had happened and the order in which it had happened, but there was something not right, something which jarred, something out of place, something which told him that this was not the open and shut case Sheila had speculated upon.

He relaxed and drew on his cigarette. It would come to him eventually.

The automatic doors swished open and a shadow fell on the whitewashed walls upon which he was leaning.

"Hello, hello, hello. What's all this 'ere, then?"

Even before he turned, Joe knew who it was. He turned and looked up several inches into a slim, lugubrious face. Brown eyes gazed from beneath a receding hairline, regarding him with curiosity and the pleasure of recognition. Beneath an aquiline nose, thin, almost cruel lips spread in a smile, which gradually broadened into a grin.

"Hello, Joe."

Joe grinned, too. Jamming his cigarette in his mouth, he offered his hand. Detective Chief Inspector Terry Cummins took it, his slender, yet powerful paw smothering Joe's.

"Great to see you again, Terry. How are you, you old scroat?"

"I'm well, Joe," Chief Inspector Cummins replied. "But you haven't put an ounce of weight on for all your meat pies, have you?"

Joe patted his non-existent belly. "Six pack."

"More like an empty party seven," Cummins replied. The

policeman fished into his pocket and came out with a pack of Benson & Hedges. He offered one to Joe who shook his head. "You still prefer your roll-ups?"

"Some things never change, Terry." Joe laughed. "So you're back in York, now?"

"I was only in Scarborough for a few weeks Joe, and we were grateful for your help in clearing up that business in Filey." Cummins lit his cigarette. "And now we have another mess. According to what I've heard already, it's an open and shut case, and I've put out the APW on Richard Hart."

"Who?" Joe asked.

"Rick Hart. The DJ. The one you saw driving away."

"Oh right. Yeah. Go on."

"I was saying, it's an apparently open and shut case. Prudhoe went across to the Old Inn, Rick brained him with the jack handle then ran for it. But then someone tells me about a missing pearl necklace and suddenly there are questions."

Joe's mind was rambling again. Cummins had just said something to trigger his memories, and once more he saw clearly the scene in the Old Inn, heard once again the roar of the diesel engine, rushed out into the rain, caught sight of it turning towards York, and heard Linda Ellis screaming after it.

Something was not right. What was it?

"Questions such as?" he asked unconsciously mimicking Brenda from a few minutes earlier.

Cummins shrugged, mirroring Joe's own reaction to the same query. "How did Rick Hart get the necklace, if, indeed, he has it? What was Palmer doing in the Old Inn? The ghost walk was over and done with anything up to half an hour previously. And, obviously, I can come up with at least one other suspect."

"Who?" Joe asked with the feeling that he already knew the answer.

"You."

Cummins' gaze was steady, but fixed, holding Joe's attention. There was no humour in the eyes, but no accusation either. It was, Joe knew, a simple statement of fact.

"Motive?" Joe asked.

"According to my information, you crossed swords with him a couple of times today."

"That's right," Joe agreed, "and if anyone deserved clubbing with a jack handle, it's him, but you know me better than that, Terry. If I was going to get rid of him, I'd get Lee to rustle up a dish of fugu and I'd be hundreds of miles away when Prudhoe ate it."

Cummins frowned. "Fugu?"

Joe smiled. "Japanese term for puffer fish and the dishes prepared from it. If it's not done correctly, it can be lethal." Joe raked his memory. "Tetrodotoxin, I think the poison is called. Japanese chefs have to be licensed to prepare it. Come on, Terry, didn't you ever read James Bond? At the end of *From Russia With Love*, Rosa Klebb pumps him full of the stuff, and early in *Dr No*, M talks to some high priced medic about it."

"You always did read too much," Cummins grumbled. "Come on then, Joe. Tell me what you have?"

"Very little," Joe confessed, and proceeded to run through the day's events for the Chief Inspector's benefit.

Cummins listened, occasionally asking questions to clarify one point or another, and when Joe was through, he summarised, "So you feel that the pearl necklace was either stolen by Yvonne Naylor and Geoff Vallance working together, or it was never in the package in the first place, meaning Edgar Prudhoe was up to something?"

"Not necessarily," Joe said. "It could be that the necklace had sat around the Prudhoe's house. He says he kept it in his safe and only he knows the combination. He also changed the combination once a month. According to him, that is. But we don't know for sure that others couldn't get into the safe. The wife, the daughter, members of his household staff, if he had any, even the boyfriend, Callum McGuire, who, I have to say, Prudhoe didn't like or trust one inch. Any one of them could have got hold of the combination and taken the necklace long before tonight."

"All right," Cummins concluded. "So what it boils down to is either a joint effort by Yvonne Naylor and Geoff Vallance, or the necklace was never actually in the package when they put it in the safe, with a number of possibilities as to why it wasn't."

Joe agreed and crushed out his cigarette. "But this is all assuming that the necklace was part of the reason he was killed."

Cummins grinned. "Who was it that told me he didn't believe in coincidence?"

"I don't," Joe agreed, "but the truth is, they happen all the time." His eyes narrowed, deep in thought. "You say you've put out an APW on Rick Hart. Does that mean you haven't actually nicked him yet?"

"Not yet," the Chief Inspector agreed, "but we'll get him." He checked the time. "It's still less than an hour since he left here. He can't get too far in that time. Say fifty, sixty miles, and every police car in North, South, and West Yorkshire is looking for him, as well as neighbouring teams in Greater Manchester, Teesside, Lincolnshire, and Derbyshire. The Bradford police have already been alerted to his home in Wibsey and his parents' place on the other side of the city."

"Ports?" Joe asked.

Cummins laughed. "Do you never learn, Joe? APW stands for all ports warning."

Joe smiled. "I was just testing." He paused a moment, once again deep in thought. "You need to tell them to search him and his vehicle thoroughly when they get him," he said.

"Stick to deduction, Joe," Cummins advised. "Don't teach me how to do my job. When they get him, both he and his vehicle will be searched before they're brought back here. Now come on, let's take a look in the Old Inn."

Collars turned up, caps pulled down against the vicious night, they strode quickly along the front of the hotel, and crossed the open car park at the rear to the Old Inn, where powerful arc lights had already been set up by the scientific support team.

Stopping by the open door, Cummins handed Joe a pair of forensic gloves. "All I ask, Joe, is you don't disturb anything."

"I know the drill, Terry. Lead on."

They stepped into the open room.

Prudhoe lay where he had died, face down on the dusty wooden floor, a police doctor bending over him, pulling bloods into a syringe. The murder weapon, having been photographed *in situ*, was now parcelled up in a large seal-easy evidence bag and lay on a table to one side, near Rick Hart's lights.

Joe scanned the room and noticed the large cupboard door on the rear wall, still open, a police officer dusting inside for fingerprints.

"Hole drilled in the door at eye level," Cummins explained. "We assume that's where the 'ghost' hides for the walk through."

"I saw his girlfriend, Linda Ellis, giving him signals while she was trying to contact the spirit of Jack Palmer." Joe said. "Haven't found anything in the cupboard, have they? Like a Zippo lighter?"

Cummins shook his head and chuckled. "You lose one?"

"No. The bloody ghost took it. And since Rick Hart is the ghost…"

"That's why you don't see him for the first half of the show," Cummins explained. He strode across to the table and picked up the murder weapon, examining it closely through the transparent bag. "You know what it is?" he asked of Joe.

"I didn't touch it, Terry, but I guessed it was a jack handle."

"Correct," Cummins agreed. He showed it to Joe: a piece of tubular steel almost three feet long, with two gouges cut into one end, each about a quarter of an inch deep, diametrically opposed to each other. "You hook the gouges onto the little lever at the side of the jack, and turn it one way to raise the jack, the other way to lower it." The Chief Inspector grinned. "This is for a bottle jack. Not a scissor jack, which is the kind you usually get with a car."

A shock of realisation ran through Joe. The little niggle was cleared up. "I'll tell you something else, Terry."

Cummins raised his eyebrows.

"You don't get a bottle jack with a van like Rick Hart's, either."

Chapter Nine

Cummins was in the act of laying the handle down again. Now his head whipped round so fast Joe could almost hear the sinews straining.

"What?" the Chief Inspector demanded. "What the hell are you saying?"

Joe nodded and rolled a cigarette. "Do you remember that old Vauxhall of mine? Must be, what, eighteen months, two years back, now, I needed some major work done on it. Short engine. I was without it for nigh on a week. As you know, I can't afford to be without a car. I need it for sandwich deliveries, urgent trips to the cash and carry and what have you. So while the Vauxhall was away for repair, I had to hire one, and the only thing the rental company had was a Ford Transit van. One of the new ones. They're smaller than they used to be and it had a scissor jack, just like a car. I remember because when I took it back, they checked it to make sure I hadn't nicked it." He moistened the cigarette paper and rolled the smoke up. "Rick Hart drives a new Transit van."

Cummins looked from him to the jack handle and back again, and Joe could understand his confusion. He, himself, had been trying to think what was out of place ever since he discovered Prudhoe's body.

"Are you telling me this didn't come from Hart's van?" Cummins demanded rapping the jack handle into his left palm.

"Nope," Joe replied. "I'm saying it's not the standard jack issued with the vehicle. Hart could have begged, stolen, or borrowed a bottle jack from someone somewhere. Maybe he keeps the jack handle for security reasons. His disco equipment is like mine, and that gear doesn't come cheap, so you need to protect it. Did your boys find any prints on it?"

Cummins consulted with a forensic officer, and then returned to Joe. "None," he said. "Wiped clean."

"That confirms what I said to Sheila and Brenda in the bar," Joe said, and went on to explain his companions' idea that it may have been a spur-of-the-moment crime. "This was premeditated. A jack handle like that should be covered in prints, particularly Hart's, but it's been cleaned up. Only someone who intended to use it on Prudhoe would go to the trouble of cleaning it first."

"Makes sense, I suppose," Cummins granted. "Joe, you were here during the ghost, er, blackout, let's call it. The minute or two when Hart turned out the lights. Was there anything unusual with Prudhoe then?"

Joe was impressed with Cummins' thoroughness. Here less than an hour and already he had familiarised himself with the course of events before, during and after the ghost walk.

"Prudhoe wasn't on the walk," he replied to the Chief Inspector's query. "His wife was, and so was his daughter, but he stayed in the bar with his prospective son-in-law. And there wasn't anything unusual during the blackout other than the jostling when Hart scared people. And he was only doing that to add to the fun and to give him an opportunity to pick a few pockets."

Cummins chewed his lip. "Yes, Linda Ellis told us about that. She was in the bar expecting Hart to come back so they could arrange to return the items. It was part and parcel of the show."

They fell into silence, watching the forensic officers at work.

"If you were here a minute or so after Prudhoe was killed, how did Hart get out?" Cummins asked.

Joe pointed to the far left corner. "Through the stables. The outer door was open when I checked it."

"I'll get some people in there."

"I shouldn't think they'll find much. The place is a bombsite. Full of old, broken bits of furniture." Joe faced Cummins. "Terry, I don't wanna tell you your job, but there's nothing we can do in here. The scene of crime is where your scientific wallahs need to be." He gestured at the forensic officers. "We need to be talking to other people; particularly the Prudhoes, Yvonne Naylor, Geoff Vallance and especially Linda Ellis."

Cummins nodded his agreement. "Come on then. I'll let you sit in on the Q&A, but remember, Joe, you have no actual authority. If they won't answer, you can't do anything about it."

Joe laughed. "No? Watch me."

They stepped out in the vicious night again and crossed the car park, making their way up to the entrance where they sheltered under the portico.

Cummins lit a cigarette. "Bad business, this. An MP murdered. You know what'll happen next, don't you? Downing Street will be onto the Home Office and they'll come down on us like a ton of bricks."

"Telling you how crap you are at your job? Yeah. I know."

"I need to clear it up quick, Joe." Cummins watched the wind lashing the trees lining the car park. "How did you find Prudhoe?"

"As a person or as a body? As a body, he was just lying there. As a person, he was arrogant, ignorant, cocksure, full of his own self-importance." Joe shrugged and drew on his smoke. "He was a bog-standard politician. He wasn't interested in anyone else's opinion or point of view but his own. Couldn't care less about the people around him or the difficulties he created for them. Bear in mind I only met him this afternoon, but if I saw him crossing the road, I'd be tempted to accelerate and mow him down. He was that kind of man."

"And someone like that is bound to have his share of enemies, isn't he?"

"More than likely," Joe agreed, "but how many of those enemies are here tonight?"

Cummins stubbed out his cigarette. "We won't know until we get on with the job."

Joe, too, put out his smoke and they walked back into the hotel.

***

Yvonne allocated a small conference room just off the reception area for Cummins to use as an interview room. Designed to hold a dozen or more people, with only Joe, the Chief Inspector, a woman constable delegated to take notes, and Linda in it, the place felt roomy. The hotel had laid on tea, coffee, soft drinks and water for the police to use and after handing a cup of tea to Linda, Cummins began his interrogation.

"Right, Ms Ellis, you know Mr Murray, don't you?"

Linda appeared still distraught. Her makeup was streaked where tears had run down her cheeks, her mouth worked worriedly, and her whole posture was hunched, tense, defensive.

She toyed nervously with an engagement ring, and did not look either man in the eye. Instead, in answer to Cummins, she merely nodded.

"I'm not a cop, Linda, but I do help them out occasionally because I have recognised powers of observation and deduction," Joe explained. "I'll tell you right now that I don't believe you're involved in the death of Edgar Prudhoe, but all the evidence points at your boyfriend, Rick Hart, so we need to know as much about him and your show as we can. You okay with that?"

Again she nodded.

"How long have you known Hart?" Cummins asked.

She cleared her throat. "About five years. We met when we were in college."

"Studying what?" the Chief Inspector asked.

"Media, er, entertainment. You know. I was doing music. Basically, I'm a singer and an actress. Rick was in my year, but he was more into comedy and specialist acts. Conjuring."

Joe leapt on the admission. "Conjuring. Stage magic?"

She nodded again. "It's highly skilled work. Rick was good at it."

"You're partners?" Cummins asked. "As in life partners, not just business."

"We live together if that's what you mean," Linda agreed.

"You make good money on this kind of gig?" Joe asked.

Linda shook her head. "Not especially. More than we would if we were filling shelves in a supermarket, but it's not brilliant. By the time we've done with equipment, props, diesel for the van, insurance and that kind of thing, we scrape a living. It's an expensive lifestyle in a lot of ways. We tend to eat out because we're always on the road, so it's not cheap."

"Tell me about it," Joe grumbled. "I get enough earache from my customers. If they knew the prices I have to pay at the wholesalers, and the cost of wages, lighting –"

"We're getting a little off track, Joe," Cummins cut in.

"Not really," Joe disagreed. "Let's be blunt, Linda, do you have money problems?"

She shrugged and swept her still damp hair out of her eyes. "No worse than anyone else. We have bills to pay, we have to live and we like to go out now and then… when we get a night off."

Cummins half turned away from her and leaned close to whisper. "I don't see where this is leading, Joe."

"The stolen necklace," Joe replied. "I said earlier, to Yvonne, Geoff and Prudhoe, that if it wasn't one of them it had to be a magician and now it turns out we had a stage magician in our midst."

"We're looking for a killer."

"No coincidences, remember?"

Cummins shrugged. "All right. You lead for a minute."

They concentrated on Linda again, Joe demanding, "Tell me how the ghost walk works."

"We do them at lots of places," she explained. "Well. About half a dozen, anyway. It was one of Rick's ideas. We find a hotel or pub that's supposed to be haunted, like The Palmer, then develop the story with the management, and organise the ghost walk. Rick susses the places out in advance, and finds somewhere to hide. Here, he uses a cupboard in the Old Inn. He drilled a hole in the door so he can kill the lights by remote…"

"The management let you set up a remote control for the lights?" Cummins asked, his voice dripping disbelief.

"They have their own lights, Terry," Joe pointed out.

Linda concurred. "We can't fool around with the main lights, so we rig our own when we get here."

"They're still in the Old Inn," Joe said for Cummins' benefit. "Rick had taken them down and they were on the table with the mur… the jack handle."

"Rick hangs a sensor on the wall," Linda explained. "In this place, we hang it near the proper lights switches. When everyone's gathered, I know exactly where to stand to keep others out of his line of sight so that he can hit the sensor with the remote. At the appropriate point in the tale, he kills the light. I mask the sound of him coming out of the cupboard by appealing to everyone to stay still. He then circles the group, and he touches one or two people. Not naughtily or anything. They usually scream. He nudges others and in the confusion, he takes things from pockets. We mark the people in advance." She aimed a shaking finger at Joe. "You were one of tonight's marks. I saw you drop an expensive cigarette lighter in the dining room, and I took note of which pocket you put it in. Rick dipped you during the confusion and stole your lighter." Her face fell. "He would have left it for you to find in the bar if… if…" She began to cry again.

109

Joe felt a wave of sympathy for the woman. Her entire life had collapsed around her in the last hour. It would feel to her like the Lazy Luncheonette burning down would to him.

"It's all right, Linda," he reassured her. "We understand how you feel." To Cummins, he said, "I told you earlier that I'd seen Linda giving signals when she was pretending to contact Jack Palmer's ghost." Concentrating once more on Linda, he said, "You gave him three signals: numbers four, six and twelve. I think they were me, Deidre Prudhoe and my friend Les Tanner, who was dressed as a soldier."

Linda nodded. "You were the three marks."

"Right," Joe said. "Afterwards, I owned up to losing my lighter, Les has lost an expensive pen. You marked me when you saw the lighter in the dining room. I'm guessing you marked Les after you saw the pen in his breast pocket. What was it about Deidre that made you mark her?"

Linda shrugged. "Nothing particular. Not like you and your friend. But she was wearing the right kind of coat. One with deep pockets. And I'd had an argument with Edgar Prudhoe earlier. The daft prat warned me to get his daughter's birthday announcement right or he'd get me fired. Christ, I don't even work here."

She was getting angry again. Joe soothed her.

"Take it easy, Linda. No need to get excited. So you're telling me you marked Deidre Prudhoe just as a way of cocking a snook at her husband?"

Linda nodded.

"Now this next question is important. How well did Rick know Edgar Prudhoe?"

"He didn't," she said through her tears. "Neither of us did. We'd never even heard of him until we got here today." Her anger began to burst through again. "That piece of garbage deserved everything he got, but I…" again, she broke down.

Cummins allowed her a moment or two to get herself together. "All right, Ms Ellis. Can you tell me, how did Rick see in the dark when he put the lights out on the ghost walk?"

She drew in a shuddery breath, like a sob catching in her throat. "He uses a night vision lens. He had it rigged up on a headset to leave his hands free. I told you, he's a professional. In his own way, he's brilliant."

"You know about the missing necklace?" Joe asked.

She nodded. "Doesn't everyone. Loudmouth let the whole sodding place know."

"Of course," Joe said. "You were there when he tried to lock the place up, weren't you. But Rick wasn't. Did he know about it?"

"Yes. I rang him while you were in the manager's office with Prudhoe. At the time, we didn't know whether The Palmer would allow the ghost walk to go ahead." Her face fell. "Now I wish they hadn't."

"Linda," Joe began cautiously, "my next question is fairly delicate, but I need an honest answer. Is there any way that Rick could have got into the manager's office today?"

She frowned. "Not without Yvonne or Geoff being there, no. Why do you ask?"

"Yes, Joe, why do you ask?" Cummins echoed.

"Rick's a conjuror," Joe explained. "Linda just said so. Stage magic isn't really magic. We all know that. It's sleight of hand. Yvonne has three keys for the safe. If Rick spotted and recognised one, he would be able to take it without her noticing. That's his art. If he then got back into her office, he could have taken the parcel, locked the safe, sneaked out to his van, removed the contents, repacked the box and bided his time to replace the empty box in the safe."

Linda's mouth fell open. "He's not a thief," she declared, the horror at such a suggestion seeping through her words.

"I have to say, Joe, it's stretching the imagination," Cummins concurred.

Joe, too, agreed. "I know it is, but so is the actual theft of the necklace." He leaned forward on the table and played with his tobacco tin. "Like any other killing we need to understand why it happened. I insist that this was premeditated, and everything points to that conclusion; the speed at which it happened, the fact that the murder weapon was clean of prints. Rick is in the hot seat right now. Why would he kill Edgar, a man he doesn't know? The only conclusion you can come to is the necklace. If he stole the necklace, if Edgar either guessed or knew Rick had stolen it, he went to the Old Inn to confront the thief. Rick had already decided he would have to dispose of Edgar when he arrived. He did so, then heard me coming in, so he ran. You say I'm stretching a point, Terry, but the whole thing beggars belief." He swung his gaze on Linda. "They'll find Rick, and I'm willing to bet they find the necklace on him, but I wouldn't put Monday's takings on him being the killer."

Linda gawped and Cummins' eyebrows shot up.

"What?" the Chief Inspector demanded. "You think he's innocent?"

"Of the killing, yes," Joe declared. "Of the theft, I don't know, but again the answer is probably yes. I think it likely that Rick has the necklace. I think he may have found it in the Old Inn, and when Prudhoe went over there, it wasn't to meet Rick, but to get the necklace back, and the killer was waiting for him. Rick realised how much trouble he could be in, and like an idiot, he panicked and ran for it."

The Chief Inspector's phone trilled for attention. He picked it up and put it to his ear. "Cummins." He listened for a few moments, his face impassive. At length, he said, "All right. We'll still be here." Killing the connection, he put the instrument down, and said, "We'll soon know. That was the Selby station. They stopped Rick Hart and his van on Doncaster Road, half an hour ago. They're loading the vehicle onto a wrecker and they're on their way here with Hart. They should be here within the next hour or two." He eyed Linda. "I'd be grateful if you'd keep yourself nearby, young lady. We may need you to persuade him to talk to us."

The Chief Inspector nodded to the constable and Linda was shown from the room.

As the door closed, he faced his old friend. "That theory was right out of left field, Joe."

"Not really," Joe argued. "The whole scenario doesn't make sense, and even if I'm right, there are still so many questions we need answered."

"Go on."

"If the necklace was in the Old Inn, how did it get there? How did Prudhoe know it was there? If the necklace wasn't in the Old Inn, why did Prudhoe go over there? At the time he left his table to walk to his death, the table where he and his family had been sitting all night was empty. Where were his wife, daughter, and her boyfriend? When I came out into Reception, neither Yvonne Naylor nor Geoff Vallance were anywhere to be seen. Where were they? In short, Terry, everyone who could be implicated in the theft, and by default, the murderer, was missing."

"And you insist that his murder was connected with the disappearance of the necklace earlier?"

Joe shrugged. "We don't have any evidence to the contrary, do we? Occam's Razor. Until we have another, definite link, don't go there."

Chapter Ten

While they waited for Rick Hart to be brought back to the hotel, Cummins ordered Yvonne Naylor to be brought in for questioning. After announcing the reason for Joe's presence, Cummins asked, "Where were you when Prudhoe left the bar to go to the Old Inn?"

"I really can't say," she replied. "Probably in the office."

"You didn't answer the Reception bell when I rang it," Joe pointed out. "No one did."

"In that case, I was probably on my break." She smiled weakly. "Our shifts tend to be very long. Midday to midnight. I hadn't had a proper break all day and I was tired. Geoff suggested I take half an hour to get some shuteye, and I did. However, Geoff should have been available if you'd wanted us, Mr Murray. If he wasn't, all I can say is, he was probably doing his rounds or something had cropped up that needed his attention."

Joe let the issue go, and eyed her malformed hand. "May I ask, Ms Naylor, how did that come about?"

Her cheeks coloured. "It's Mrs Naylor, and this," she held up her hand, "is something I prefer not to talk about."

"Was it down to the same fire that killed your husband?" Joe asked and her face registered surprise.

"How did you guess?"

Joe gave her a superior smile. "Not guesswork, deduction. You told me earlier that it had happened in a fire and you said you were lucky to only lose your hand. Just now you stressed the point that you are *Mrs* Naylor, not Ms. You also said you prefer not to talk about the incident. That means it was pretty traumatic. If you were divorced, you'd probably want to forget he ever existed, and you wouldn't have objected. Only a woman who valued her marriage and had lost her husband would correct me. I figured he was either dead or so incapacitated by the fire that he may as well be."

"Very clever," Yvonne said with a withering stare, "and quite correct. My husband and I ran our own pub in East Anglia. An old, Georgian building. Listed. We didn't own the place, we managed it on behalf of the brewery. During a routine inspection by the Health & Safety people, a few structural problems were brought to our attention. We, naturally, reported back to the brewery, and they promised to deal with the matter. But they were in no hurry, and we guessed that they were considering selling it off or even leaving it to rot. About a month later, the place caught fire. Ron and I were asleep upstairs. We came out of the bedroom when the alarms went off, but the smoke held us back and the staircase was already alight. We were trapped, Mr Murray. Ron smashed a window and we jumped for it. I got clear and Ron landed behind me. At that moment, half the front of the building came down, still blazing, and trapped him by the legs. I took hold of his hand and tried to drag him out. I couldn't. The flames came too close to me and my hand was badly burned." A shudder ran through her. "To this day, every time I look at this hand, I can hear his screams as he burned to death under those timbers." She held up the hand again. "I lost a finger and I lost the use of this hand. I got off lightly, and do you know something? So did the brewery. They were fined ten thousand pounds for their failure to meet the requirements of the Health and Safety at Work Act. But they had relieved themselves of some potentially expensive renovation work, and obviously there were the usual rumours flying around that the HSE inspectors had been bought off, and that the fire was deliberate."

"Any proof of that?" Joe asked.

"Of course not. According to the Fire Brigade Inspectors, the fire was started by faulty wiring in the cellars." Yvonne glowered. "I lost a hand, I lost my husband, English Heritage lost a fine example of Georgian, rural architecture, the brewery took a smack on the wrist and got rid of a liability. Now do you understand why I don't like to talk about it?"

"Perfectly," Joe replied. "And the brewery in question?"

"Billington's," she told him. "They were well known in East Anglia."

"Were?" Joe asked.

"They went under about four years ago. Bought out by a firm of asset strippers."

Joe nodded. "And what was the pub called, again?"

"The Ferryman. Near Hunstanton, North Norfolk." Yvonne's eyes narrowed again. "Is there a point to all these questions, Mr Murray?"

"I don't know," Joe admitted. "I'm trying to build a picture of you, so I can decide whether or not you murdered Edgar Prudhoe."

Outrage shot across her already angry features. "Murdered Edgar... How dare you suggest..."

"Someone has to, Yvonne," Joe interrupted. "I caught you arguing with Prudhoe earlier today. He threatened your job, your livelihood. Whether he could get away with that, I don't know, but even if he could, it would be a pretty thin reason for killing him. Much better to show him up in public. But I like to exercise my mind on narrow strands of possibility. Suppose for a minute that Edgar Prudhoe was a major shareholder in Billington's Brewery at the time the Ferryman burned down? Suppose he also used his Parliamentary influence to keep the Health and Safety Executive off the brewery's back? It's stretching a point, but you may just see him as liable for both the loss of your husband and your infirmity."

"I see." The severity of her mood punctuated her words.

"Well let me hasten to disabuse you. The Ferryman burned down almost fifteen years ago. Long before Edgar Prudhoe became an MP, and as far as I'm aware, he had no dealings with the brewery. And while there were rumours that the HSE had been bought off, or pressured into silence, I never subscribed to them. You're a businessman, you should know that every time there's a major event like that, these kind of tales soon spread."

Joe shrugged. "Okay." He looked at Cummins. "Terry."

The Chief Inspector, who had watched the exchange with a mixture of emotions from humour to amazement to shock, checked his own notes.

"Now, Mrs Naylor, for the moment we're working on the theory that Mr Prudhoe's death was linked to the theft of the necklace he left in your safe. Rick Hart has been arrested and he's being brought back here as we speak. On the face of it, he is our killer, but both Mr Murray and I have our doubts. At some stage, madam, I'll have to ask you to account for your precise movements between the end of the ghost walk and the discovery of Mr Prudhoe's body; a period of about thirty minutes. If you could concentrate on that when we're finished, I'd be grateful. In the meantime, may I ask how well do you know Rick Hart and Linda Ellis?"

"I don't." Yvonne replied. "I haven't been here that long. I transferred from London about four weeks ago."

"The company sent you here?" Cummins asked.

"I applied for the post," she said. "The previous manager left in August. I've been with Accomplus for the last ten years. I was Deputy Reservations Manager at the head office in Hammersmith. I thought it was time I moved up another notch, and before moving to London, I'd put in my share of time on Reception at a number of sites, so I applied for The Palmer and got it. Linda and Rick put on the ghost walk once a month and I arrived here on the Saturday afternoon as they appeared on the Saturday night. I was too busy that day to do anything other than introduce myself. I didn't really get to meet them until this morning when they arrived. Geoff knows them much better than I do."

"We'll speak to Mr Vallance in due course," Cummins said. "What was your impression of them?"

"Capable," Yvonne replied without hesitation. "They've put this gig on for the last year and a half as I understand it, so they know the drill. The size of the audience varies month by month, and tonight we had to close the show to non-residents because of the numbers involved from the Sanford Third Age Club. Linda and Rick know exactly what they're doing, and the moment they arrived, they had a quick drink and a bite to eat in the bar before setting up the show."

"Linda was telling us. It's a complicated job," Joe commented.

"From our point of view, yes," Yvonne agreed, "but it's meat and veg' to Linda and Rick because they've done it for so long."

"How did you find Rick?" Joe persisted.

"I barely spoke to him. He appears a little, shall we say, carefree. He treats life as a joke. I'm not questioning his entertainment skills, his talent, but his approach could be a little more serious."

"Did you know he was a conjuror?"

Her eyes opened wide. "I'd seen him do silly little party tricks, but I didn't realise he a professional illusionist, no. Is it significant?"

"It might be," Joe suggested, "if we think about the theft of the necklace."

Yvonne pouted. "You know my opinion of that, Mr Murray."

"Tell me your opinion, Mrs Naylor," Cummins insisted.

She cleared her throat. "I think Prudhoe was pulling a scam. I think that box was empty when he deposited it with us."

"What leads you to that conclusion?" the Chief Inspector asked.

Yvonne sounded quite definite. "To begin with, there is no way anyone could have got into that safe. I can see where Mr

Murray is leading with his point about Rick being a conjuror, but I maintain there is no way he could have got the key to the safe, and even if he did, there is no way the office was ever vacant long enough for him to get in and play about with the package. If you further assume that he simply stole it, and replaced it with another, I say that is nonsense. He would need to know in advance what the parcel looked like, and from the conversations I've had with Linda, he didn't even know Prudhoe existed until today. If you're going to suggest that he stole the package, took the necklace out and rewrapped it, he would then need another opportunity to get into the office and the safe, and he would have to leave the keys where he found them. I checked and none of the keys were missing. I also stressed to Mr Murray earlier, that as a security measure, the location of the keys is known only to myself and Geoff, and they are not on show."

"So Hart would have needed inside help," Joe said and Yvonne bristled again.

"I know I didn't help him and I trust Geoff completely."

"Your opinion is based on nothing more than the impossibility of getting the keys," Joe complained, "and I say there is always a way."

She shook her head. "That's not strictly accurate, Mr Murray. There's something else." She paused a moment ensuring that she had their attention. "When he signed the package back out, Prudhoe insisted that he was signing it 'unexamined'. You're the famous amateur detective, Joe Murray, so how would you interpret that?"

Joe declined to answer with a shake of the head.

"We're more interested in how you would interpret it, Mrs Naylor," Cummins pointed out.

"Let's assume you give me your wallet and ask me to keep it in the safe. What's the first thing you'll do when you sign it out again? You'll check that the contents are all there. Now, suppose you give me a sealed package. What will you do with that when you sign it back out? You won't check that the contents are all there because you know they *must be* there. So did Prudhoe simply assume that someone would make an effort to steal his precious bloody necklace while it was in our care? Or was he covering his backside for a claim on his insurance?"

"If he was, it was a clumsy way to go about it," Joe commented, "because as you say, it would arouse suspicion."

Yvonne scowled. "He was a politician, Mr Murray. No one said he was intelligent."

***

Repeating his request for the manager to write out a detailed account of her movements during the relevant half hour, Cummins allowed Yvonne to leave and while waiting for Geoff, talked with Joe.

"My guess is she won't have done it," he said.

Joe went so far to agree. "Probably not, but you never cross anyone off the list until you're absolutely sure. How well do you know the next guy, Geoff Vallance?"

"Local lad, ran his own business for some years, supplying disability aids, but went out of business when his premises were bought by compulsory purchase order. Not one I would have considered a run of the mill killer, but again, you never know."

As Cummins promised, when interviewed, Geoff could throw no light on either the theft of the necklace, or the murder.

"I think the theft was a scam," he declared, "and at the time of the killing, I was on the third floor, persuading the lifts to work."

"Bit menial, that kind of work, isn't it?" Joe asked.

"This is a small hotel, Mr Murray, and we're out in the sticks," Geoff responded. "To call out an engineer at this time on a Saturday night would cost a fortune, so we don't unless we really have to. As it happens it was a cigarette packet that had been dropped and got trapped in the door preventing it closing properly. As you must know, if the doors won't close, the lifts won't work. It was a simple enough job. I just switched off the lifts for a few minutes, prised the cigarette packet out, and then switched them back on again. They worked perfectly after that, and I probably saved the hotel three or four hundred pounds."

"Can anyone confirm your whereabouts, Mr Vallance?" Cummins asked.

"No. Do I need anyone to confirm it?"

"I don't know," Cummins admitted. "If you do, we'll let you know."

"Cummins tells me you used to have your own business," Joe said. "Went under after the property was bought out."

"That's correct."

"Angry, were you?"

"Yes," Geoff confessed, "but I don't see what that has to do with tonight's events."

"Well, see, I'm in a similar position to the one you used to be in," Joe declared. "I own my place, I don't rent, but if the council ever decide to pull the place down, I'll get less than market value and I don't know if I'll be able to set up again. If it happened, I'd be pretty mad at our local politicians."

Geoff smiled. "Ah. I see. You think I may have been mad at our local politicians. Mad enough to kill them. Well, you're probably right, but it still doesn't tie in with Edgar Prudhoe's death."

"Oh yes it does," Joe disagreed. "You're an intelligent man. When your local wallahs decided to pull down your premises, you must have appealed, and sometimes those appeals go to inquiries and MPs can hold a lot of sway with them. Is that what happened to you?"

"Very perceptive, Mr Murray," Geoff congratulated him. "Yes, there was a public inquiry, and scuttlebutt insisted that a cross party group of MPs put pressure on the inquiry to find in favour of the developers. We traders were all ready to believe that, and one of those mentioned was Edgar Prudhoe. However, his was only one of eight or nine names being bandied about. Obviously, there was never any proof, and I didn't set out to kill any of the others, so why should I decide to murder Prudhoe?"

"Because he was here," Joe suggested.

"Nice try, but wrong," Geoff insisted. "You don't hurt men like Prudhoe by killing them. It's too good. You hurt them by making them suffer. By all accounts Prudhoe never knew what hit him. No, sir, if I was out to kill him, I would have made it a long, slow and tortuous process. I would want him to regret the day he was born before giving him the benefit of extinction."

Dismissed, as Yvonne had been, with instructions to detail his movements, Cummins and Joe conferred again.

"He had a strong reason to hate the Prudhoes of this world as a breed," the Chief Inspector pointed out.

"But was it strong enough to kill him?" Joe asked.

Cummins' mobile interrupted and there followed several minutes while Cummins listened more than he talked and when he did speak, it amounted to nothing more than, 'yes, sir', 'no, sir', and 'I fully understand that, sir'.

Eventually, he closed the phone, his ears burning. "The Chief Constable," he explained. "The Home Secretary has already been onto him and as I forecast, she's made it plain that Downing Street expects an early arrest."

"Regardless of guilt or innocence?" Joe asked. "Politicians. Who'd have 'em?"

"I told you. I've been expecting that call since we first heard Prudhoe had been killed. Let's get back to work. The Prudhoe family."

Of the three family members, Hannah was still too distressed to offer any evidence, and when she was called in, Deidre was too drunk. Only Cal had anything serious to say.

"I don't know who killed him," he said, "but I do know why he went to the Old Inn. He was expecting to meet me there."

Both Cummins and Joe were surprised. "Why?" the Chief Inspector asked.

"He didn't like me," Cal admitted. "He wanted me away from his daughter. Earlier today, he and I had a chat in the bar. He told me to be at the Old Inn after the ghost walk and it would be worth £10,000 to me, provided I got away from his daughter."

Joe whistled. "You're right, he didn't like you. I'd have to seriously hate someone to offer that much to be rid of them. How would the ten grand be paid? Cash?"

Cal shrugged. "Haven't a clue because we didn't go into it. He just told me to meet him there."

"So what happened when you met him?" Cummins asked.

"Nothing happened, because I didn't go to meet him. I was in the bar all night."

Joe shook his head. "When I stood up to follow Prudhoe, your table was empty. There was no sign of you, your girlfriend, or Deidre Prudhoe."

"I was probably at the bar, or maybe the toilets. I can't say where Deidre or Hann would be, but they may have gone to the ladies."

"Did you know what Edgar Prudhoe had bought his daughter for her birthday?" Cummins pressed.

"No. He told no one. I imagine Deidre knew, but she never said anything. Mind, she rarely talks to anyone. She's usually too drunk to hold a sensible conversation."

"Getting back to Prudhoe trying to buy you off," Joe demanded, "you weren't interested?"

"Hann is what matters to me, Mr Murray, not money."

"But, obviously, now that Prudhoe is dead, Hannah will come into a lot more than ten grand, won't she? And if you marry her –"

Cal leapt to his feet. "Say one more word and –"

The uniformed policewoman half rose as Cummins cut in on Cal. "Sit down, son. There'll be no violence here. Like it or not, Mr Murray is making a valid point."

His anger barely under control, Cal sat down and hissed, "I

am not interested in Hann's inheritance. I don't even know if she has anything coming. I'm in my final year at university. When I graduate, I'll move into the I.T. sector, and ten years from now I should be making more money than Edgar Prudhoe could ever dream about."

"Ten years is a long time, kiddo," Joe told him. "I know. I was married for ten years, and it was nothing short of hell. It must be even worse when you're relying on the woman for your income." Joe drummed his fingers on the table. "Do you own a car?"

"I have a Land Rover," Cal admitted.

"What kind of jack do you have on it? Scissor jack?"

The youngster frowned. "What kind of question is that?"

"Just answer, please, McGuire," Cummins ordered.

"It came with a scissor jack, yes, but I have a bottle jack. I like to do a little off-roading in my spare time. Scissor jacks can be notoriously unreliable when you're in the middle of a field of mud."

"Where do you keep it?" Joe asked. "The jack, I mean?"

"In the back of the truck. Where else?" Cal's features became concerned, as if he felt he was being led along a path he did not want to follow. "Look, what is this?"

"What's the back flap like on your vehicle?" Joe persisted. "Solid door or a canvas flap?"

"Canvas. I don't leave anything of value in it. Will you please tell me what are you getting at?"

"Prudhoe owned a Bentley," Joe explained. "I can't be certain, but I think they come with a bottle jack as standard, so we'll need to check the boot of his car. You own a Land Rover with a canvas flap for a back door, and by your own admission, you have it equipped with a bottle jack. Do you know where the handle is for the jack right now?"

Cal shrugged again. "In the back of the truck… I hope."

"Again, we'll need to check, but I don't think so, I think it's in a police evidence bag, covered in Prudhoe's blood and brains."

Chapter Eleven

Asked to identify the murder weapon, Cal could not. "It might be mine, it might not be. There's nothing particularly outstanding about my jack handle."

Donning coats and hats again, they made their way out to the car park and even before they arrived at his Land Rover, Cal registered something was amiss.

"The flap's unfastened," he said, pointing out the canvas flailing in the wind. He hurried across, caught the flap, lifted it out of the way, and leaned in. A second later, he recoiled with a curse. "Gone. The bloody jack handle has gone."

"At least we know where the weapon came from," Joe said, "even if we don't know who took it and used it."

"Mr McGuire," Cummins said, "I'm going to need a detailed account of your movements between the end of the ghost walk and the time Mr Prudhoe's body was discovered."

"But I already told you. I never left the bar."

"I said a *detailed* account, sir. I want to know where you were every minute of that half hour."

They watch him trudge back to the hotel, an angry, yet forlorn figure.

"Well, Joe, any thoughts?"

"Yes. I think it's time I had a smoke."

They, too, made for the hotel entrance, where Joe refused one of Cummins' cigarettes, quickly rolled one of his own, lit it, and puffed out a lungful of smoke with a satisfied hiss.

"It's too early to say anything, really," he said at last. "We need to speak to Rick Hart, see what he can tell us. Right now, it would be so easy to jump to the wrong conclusion. Hart killed him after taking the handle from McGuire's Land Rover. McGuire has a beautiful motive, but it's a bit obvious. Let's not forget we haven't spoken to Hannah or Deidre Prudhoe yet, and although both may seem like outsiders, you still have to consider Yvonne and Geoff. Both had reason to hate figures of authority, both fell out with Prudhoe during the day, both may just have been angry enough to follow him and kill him, and we can't really confirm where either of them were at the time." Joe frowned. "In fact, we don't know where any of the suspects were at the time."

"It's a tough one, Joe," the Chief Inspector agreed, "but my money is still on Hart." He checked the time. "Midnight. Our resident DJ should be here any time now."

Joe took another drag on his cigarette. "I'll go check in with my crowd. Sheila and Brenda will be missing me. Gimme a shout when your boys get here with Hart."

"Will do."

Walking back to the bar, Joe passed Les Tanner and Sylvia Goodson arm in arm, heading for the lift.

"Exciting night, Murray," Tanner congratulated him.

"Not for Edgar Prudhoe," Joe pointed out. "You haven't got your pen back, yet?"

"Sheila has assured me the police will have it," Tanner replied.

"Well, I hope they have my lighter, too. You two had enough?"

"Sheila and Brenda are good on the stage, Joe," Sylvia said, "but they're not a patch on you. And we're getting old and tired."

With a good-humoured grunt, Joe bid them goodnight and wandered into the bar. "Not too old for nookie, though," he muttered to himself, and then dismissed the thought as simple envy. "Time you got yourself a girlfriend, Joe." He thought of the earlier incident with Brenda and promptly dropped the idea again. "Maybe I should find someone who's easy and just looking for a bit of excitement now and then," he murmured as he entered the bar.

The crowd had thinned out. Brenda and George Robson were dancing to Nina Simone's recording of *I Put a Spell On You*, while Sheila sat at the DJ's console chatting to Mavis Barker and Julia Staines. In the far corner, where they had been all evening, Deidre and Hannah Prudhoe sat with Cal, the daughter taking comfort from the boyfriend while the widowed mother sat in what appeared to be a drunken stupor.

"It's not an appearance, Joe," Mavis reported. "It's genuine. She's smashed out of her brains."

"Very polite, Mavis," Julia applauded.

"Polite?"

"It's not like you to use such moderate language as 'smashed'."

Julia and Sheila tittered, Mavis guffawed, and Joe drank off the remains of a half pint of bitter which had gone flat at least an hour earlier.

With Nina Simone coming to an end, Sheila switched to Frankie Laine's *Ghost Riders in the Sky*, and as the music and dancers perked up. Both Julia and Mavis went off, Julia to find her husband, Mavis on the hunt for a dance partner.

"What progress?" Sheila asked.

"None," Joe confessed. "Or so little it may as well be none." He gave her a rundown of the questioning sessions.

"So we know where the murder weapon came from," she summarised, "but we still don't know who wielded it."

"That's about the size of it. Anything happen in here?"

Sheila shook her head. "The Prudhoes have kept to themselves. I noticed one or two of our members going across there now and then. Probably offering their condolences. I saw Les and Sylvia there, earlier. The young man appears to be doing all the talking for them."

"He's the only one who's making sense," Joe agreed, and frowned. "The whole thing doesn't make much sense. We know now why Prudhoe went to the Old Inn. It was to meet McGuire. But why would Rick Hart kill him?"

"The necklace?" Sheila speculated as Brenda and George left the dance floor together.

"Come again?" Joe asked, keeping his eye on the two STAC members now making their way to the bar.

"If you believe Yvonne, Geoff and young Callum McGuire, the chances are that the necklace was never in the safe, but in Prudhoe's pocket all the time."

Joe snapped his fingers in sudden realisation. "And that was the ten grand Prudhoe was going to offer McGuire. Of course. Why didn't I think of it sooner?"

"But Callum never went," Sheila reminded him. "Instead, Prudhoe met Rick Hart who killed him for the necklace."

"Two problems," Joe said, now watching Brenda and George split, Brenda coming towards them with a small tray of drinks. "When did Rick get hold of the jack handle, which we now know came from McGuire's Land Rover?"

"I think he had plenty of time between the end of the ghost walk and Prudhoe going over there."

"He did," Joe agreed as a cheerful Brenda joined them and passed him another half of bitter. "But the bigger question is, how did Rick know that Prudhoe had the necklace in his pocket?"

"Simple," Brenda said as Sheila brought her up to speed. "Prudhoe was a loudmouth. He was always shouting the odds, and Rick could have overheard the conversation with Callum in the bar earlier today and put two and two together."

Sipping on fresh beer, Joe tossed the possibility over in his mind. "It's not likely," he said while Sheila switched tracks again, this time opting for *Witchcraft* by Sarah Vaughan.

"These tunes are getting a bit obvious," Brenda complained.

"Rick and Linda left a playlist," Sheila protested. "I'm just following it. Joe, you were saying Brenda's idea was unlikely."

"Hmm, yeah. Prudhoe may have been a loudmouth, but he wasn't stupid. Whatever little scheme he was cooking up, it was hardly on the level, and he would have kept quiet about it. Remember, he didn't even tell McGuire what the bottom line was, only its cash value." Joe yawned. "I could do with sleeping it off, clear my head, but Cummins is expecting Hart back anytime now."

Across the room, Hannah and Cal helped Deidre to her feet and out of the room. Couples on the dance floor thinned out even further, and the room gradually began to empty. Linda came in, thanked Sheila and Brenda for their efforts, but refused to look at Joe while she set about shutting down the equipment.

"Always the last to leave, the Sanford Third Age Club," Brenda commented.

"Not quite," Sheila pointed out, and nodded at Yvonne Naylor waiting at the bar for the night's takings. "She must put some hours in, that woman."

"She told me she's supposed to finish at midnight." Joe yawned again. "It goes with the territory, but quite frankly, she'd be better off if she owned the place." He drained his glass. "Time I was hitting the sack. I'll see you both at breakfast."

Ambling out into the lobby, he met Cummins.

"Ah. Joe. Change of plan. The Selby crew got waylaid by the weather. Couple of trees down on the A19. It's getting seriously late, so I told them to take Hart to the station in York. I'll question him first thing in the morning, then, unless I'm charging him, I'll bring him here."

"So you're on your way home, too?"

The Chief Inspector nodded.

"Probably for the best," Joe agreed. "We all need a decent night's kip. I'll catch you tomorrow morning, Terry."

Five minutes later, back in his room, Joe switched on his netbook and, while waiting for it to go through its start routine, he made a cup of tea. As usual, throughout the questioning, he had taken no notes, preferring to rely upon his near-eidetic memory.

"Notes," he once told a group of whodunit enthusiasts he had been invited to address, "tend to be short, almost cryptic, and if too long elapses between making the note and re-reading it, you never know what blind alleys they may lead you along. I prefer to rely on memory of the actual interview."

Which was fine when you were addressing a group of fiction fans in Sanford Public Library, but not when you had come to the end of a long day, you had been drinking, and you were in a state of physical exhaustion.

Connecting to the internet via the hotel's free wi-fi service, he first checked on Geoff Vallance's tale and after some searching through archives of local newspapers, found it. As Geoff had said, everything was down to a public inquiry which took three months to reach a decision, and then found in favour of the developers. Geoff and one or two of his fellow shopkeepers were quoted as blaming local politicians, who had always been in favour of the development. Westminster rated a mention only in passing, and even then, the comment came from one of Geoff's neighbours, not the man himself.

It was a similar story with Yvonne Naylor. He found details on a local news site of the way the Ferryman had burned down, and Yvonne had been telling the truth when she said there were allegations of bribery, but the accusations came from bog-standard fringe bloggers, those who hung around the Web, dreaming up conspiracy theories on everything from UFOs to the wholesale price of meat and potato pies. No one took the allegations seriously. Not even Yvonne. Her husband's death could not be directly attributed to the crumbling timbers of the pub, so Billington's Brewery were not held responsible, and the fire had started not from old wiring, as Joe had initially surmised, but from a new installation by a company called Anglian Electrical Contractors. Like the brewery, although they were responsible for the fire, they could not be held accountable for Ronnie Naylor's death, which, the coroner ruled, was accidental and stemmed from an unlikely series of events: the fire, the chosen escape route and the building collapsing at precisely the moment it did.

"Edgar Prudhoe's death was due to a series of unlikely events, too," Joe muttered as he turned his attention to Deidre Prudhoe.

To his surprise, a search for Deidre Prudhoe, in her own right, turned up more results than those identifying her as Edgar's wife. On one page, he found a full biography for her. Born in Fakenham, Norfolk, the daughter of a millionaire businessman, she was Deidre Hecklington (a name which Joe knew would have got her some stick in secondary school) before she became Deidre Prudhoe. Joe soon learned that she never went to secondary school... well, not the kind he went to, anyway. She had been privately educated from the age of five, and had eventually become Head Girl at an exclusive school for girls near Beccles in Norfolk. After leaving school, she spent a few years wandering around Europe, the States and the Caribbean before daddy paired her with the upwardly mobile Prudhoe.

It was a marriage which, reading between the lines, Deidre did not want, but she had been brought up by the maxim 'daddy knows best', so she acquiesced. It was shortly after that she picked up her first drink driving conviction. After two more such convictions, she was spared a jail sentence only on condition that she handed in her licence and never drove again until she had been treated for her dependency. Joe could find no record of any such treatment or of Deidre ever being charged with drunk driving again.

Suspicion began to grow in his mind. A woman in an arranged marriage, under the regime of a bullying man for so many years. Was it possible? *He's a good provider.* Deidre's words rang through Joe's head. Hadn't Brenda said the same about him? And hadn't Brenda said that he would be anything but the perfect husband? Couldn't that argument also be applied to Edgar Prudhoe? A good provider but a poor husband. The insurance, and all those millions lying in the bank, would provide just as well for her, while eliminating the problems associated with crap husbands.

It did not seem likely. Deidre Prudhoe appeared smashed out of her brains down in the bar, and she had been swaying during the ghost walk. And yet, when Joe had spoken with her earlier, she came across as stone-cold sober, so it begged the question; was the drunkenness an act? Her driving convictions indicated she did have a dependency problem, so she would know precisely how to act the part of a drunk while remaining sober.

His mind swung around the various questions without answers, and homed in on Deidre during the ghost walk. She said nothing when he and Les Tanner had owned up. Was it because nothing had been taken, as Linda had almost suggested, or was it because…

With blinding insight, Joe realised why she had not said anything, and he smiled at the ceiling. She *couldn't* say anything. Not until she got back to Edgar and told him that the necklace was missing.

After making a few notes, he shut down the computer, finished his tea, then showered and with the time coming up to two, he climbed into bed.

Lying there with the lights out, listening to the October winds buffeting the hotel, staring at the ceiling, he waited for his mind to relax. Was he missing something? In the welter of information that had come his way over the last few hours, it would be strange if he was not, but he knew the something he was missing was important. Tiny, insignificant, but trying to tell him exactly where he should be looking.

Chapter Twelve

The rain had eased but the winds still had not died down when Joe joined Sheila and Brenda for breakfast in the dining room at 9 a.m. After helping himself to bacon and eggs and a cup of strong tea, he sat between his companions and tucked in.

"Solved it, maestro?" Brenda asked with a gaping yawn.

"Shut your mouth, there's a bus coming," Joe retorted. "And, no, I haven't solved it. I need to speak to Deidre Prudhoe."

"We also need to worry about whether the police will let us all leave, Joe," Sheila pointed out. "Keith is due here with the bus between ten and eleven, and everyone in this room is a potential witness."

"Is there any rush?" Brenda asked.

"The hotel will want us out," Joe told her, "and the danger is, if we don't go, they'll bill us."

Brenda grinned lasciviously. "Get your wallet out, Joe. Better yet, give your wallet to me. I'll show it what freedom's all about."

"I could also do with speaking to Rick Hart," Joe declared as if Brenda had not said a word.

"Well, that shouldn't be too difficult to arrange," Sheila told him. "Terry Cummins has just walked in with him."

Joe looked over his shoulder to find Cummins and the young DJ weaving their way through the tables towards him.

Linda intercepted them. She launched herself at her boyfriend, but Cummins intervened and from his body language he was telling her to back off. Linda argued, Hart

134

argued, but Cummins remained firm and, at length, Linda returned to her table. Almost dragging Hart along, Cummins continued his journey through the room until he stood alongside their table.

"Terry Cummins as was," Brenda greeted him with a broad grin. "You don't remember me, do you?"

"Yes I do, Brenda. And you, Sheila. How are you both? Well, I hope."

"Well enough to keep trying for Joe's wallet," Brenda laughed, and Cummins took a seat beside her, while Rick Hart sat opposite Joe.

With the Chief Inspector and his two female companions engaged in nostalgic banter, recalling the good old days of Sanford, Joe chewed his way through rubbery eggs and bacon, occasionally glancing across at Hart.

The young man looked a forlorn figure. He had not washed, nor shaved, he was damp, his eyelids hung heavy and the eyes behind them were empty, devoid of emotion. His clothing, too, looked damp and shabby, hanging on his thin frame like loose sacks.

Suppressing any sympathy he may have felt, Joe asked, "You eaten?"

"No. Harrow." Hart gave him a lopsided grin that was obviously false.

Joe pointed a threatening fork at him. "Don't take the mick with me, lad. You're knee deep in it right now, and you don't even have a shovel, never mind a bucket. The only thing that stands between you and a murder charge is me. Now, do you want something to eat?"

Hart shook his head. "They gave me some crud in the police cells."

Joe pushed his plate away and swilled down the last of his tea. "How did you come by the necklace?"

The question signalled an end to the ribald conversation going on around him. Cummins' eyebrows shot up, Sheila and

Brenda paid sharp attention, and Rick, too, appeared surprised.

"That was a bloody good guess, Joe," the Chief Inspector said. "I haven't told anyone."

"I worked it out in the early hours," Joe replied picking his teeth and rattling his cup into the saucer. "He didn't kill Prudhoe. I'm sure he didn't. To do so he would have needed a motive, and he didn't have one. The only way he could have killed Prudhoe was in an argument, and he didn't have time for one between the Right Honourable prat showing up and me. But our friend here still ran. Why? Because there was evidence on him that might incriminate him. What might that be? We know it wasn't the murder weapon because we found that. The only other thing it could be was the necklace." He rounded on Rick again. "I know how you got it, but suppose you tell me so that my friends here don't just think I'm a smartarse."

"I dipped it," Rick replied. "Linda must have told you that I'm a member of the Magic Circle; a professional conjuror." He wriggled his hands before Joe. "Sleight of hand, and I'm an expert dip; a pickpocket. I have to be. During the blackout, I took your lighter, I took a pen from the old soldier; that pal of yours dressed as the Duke of Wellington, and I took a plastic bag from a woman's coat pocket. I didn't think anything of it at first, but when I was sorting out after the ghost walk, I checked the bag and the necklace was inside."

"It figures," Joe said and pushed his plate to one side. "Do you smoke, Hart?"

Rick shook his head.

Joe took out his tobacco tin and began to roll a cigarette. "You're gonna get cold at the front door, then, so I'd wrap up if I were you." He stood up. "Come on."

With Cummins alongside, they made their way from the dining room to the hotel entrance where Joe and Cummins lit cigarettes.

"Joe," the Chief Inspector asked, "What did you mean when you said, 'it figures'?"

"You remember McGuire told us Prudhoe wanted to pay him off? Well, that was the pay off. Prudhoe probably planned it weeks ago. The necklace was never in the package, but Prudhoe couldn't be found with it in his possession or he would be in schtum, so he gave it to an accomplice who had it in her pocket all the time. The idea was the accomplice would leave it at the Old Inn. Then, after the ghost walk, Prudhoe would go over there, retrieve the necklace, meet McGuire, and hand the goods over. McGuire would then disappear with a necklace worth fifteen grand, for which he'd get ten on the black market, Prudhoe would claim on the insurance, and only Hannah would be left crying when she learned what a thieving git McGuire was."

Joe took a deep drag on his cigarette.

"So what happened?" Cummins asked.

Joe pointed at Rick. "Prudhoe never reckoned on sonny Jim, here, nicking the necklace from his accomplice's pocket. My guess is, the accomplice went back to the bar, and when Prudhoe asked, she told him she couldn't leave the necklace because she didn't have it anymore. Prudhoe was then knee deep in the S-H-one-T with Environmental Health calling his cleaning procedures into question. If Rick, here, comes back to the bar with the necklace, the plan is shot. Worse than that, with Yvonne in the mood she was in, an inquiry might uncover the whole scam. So Prudhoe set off to the Old Inn to find either the necklace or Rick." He stared Rick in the eye. "You took it from Deidre Prudhoe, didn't you?"

Rick nodded. "I think it was her. Red anorak."

"Think, my eye. You know it was her." Joe nodded. "I saw the signals your girlfriend gave you. I was number four, Deidre was number six and Les Tanner – the old solider – was number twelve." Joe felt his blood boiling again. He rounded on Rick. "What the hell were you thinking, lad, when you ran for it?"

"What do you think I was thinking?" Rick squealed. "Prudhoe was dead on the floor, I had his bloody necklace in my pocket. I knew what it would look like and I panicked, man. I ran for it."

Joe shook his head. "The ghost walk was over half an hour before Prudhoe came across there. You had ample time to come back to the hotel and hand the necklace in." Waiting for an answer, he puffed on his cigarette.

"I was pulling the lights down. I didn't even check the haul until I was through with that job."

Joe narrowed an intense stare on him. "Quit trying to bull your way out of it. Tell the truth."

Rick's face fell, his shoulders sagged, and he sighed. "All right, all right, so I was thinking of running with the goods. Look, man, do you know what it's like to be short of cash? Linda and me, we do all right, but we're always short of money. Not hard up, just short. Y'know? An extra ton a week would see us in easy street, but that ton is never there. Then suddenly, I have hold of this necklace which I know to be worth a few thou', and I thought, 'your lucky night, Rick. Get the hell out while you can'. I tried to ring Linda, but she couldn't hear me for the noise of the disco, so I sat in the Old Inn thinking about it."

"One or two of my members heard Linda shouting at him down the phone," Joe confirmed for Cummins' benefit.

"Eventually, I decided it was time to leave," Rick concluded his tale, "but before I could, Prudhoe turned up."

"You spoke to him?" Cummins asked.

"No way, man." Rick shook his head. "That tosser would have had me locked up. I got back into my cupboard and lay low. I figured he'd come to look for the necklace. Then I heard the thump on his head, I heard him fall, and I heard someone running out through the stables. I came out of my cupboard and I saw Prudhoe lying there, and I thought, 'yeah, good deal. I'm out of here, too'. Then I heard the door again." He looked at Joe. "It was you. And that's when I ran."

"The place was in total darkness," Joe said. "How did you see

Prudhoe lying there?"

"Night vision lens," Rick replied. "The filth have it in York."

"The filth don't have it in York, lad," Cummins bristled. "I have it in my car. Along with your lighter, Joe, and Les Tanner's pen."

Joe smiled his gratitude. To Rick, he said, "So you saw the killer too?"

"No. I was in the cupboard crouched down. I have a hole drilled in the door at eye level, but I was keeping my head down. I heard everything, though. The killer didn't make a sound, and neither did Prudhoe when he got hit. I heard him fall, I heard the iron bar hit the floor, I heard the killer running for it."

Joe chewed on his cigarette for a moment. Then he took a drag before crushing it out. "Terry, are your forensic boys finished over there?"

"They've done the bulk of the work, yes."

"Can we go over?"

Cummins considered it a moment. "Why?"

"I need to get a few things straight in my head."

Again Cummins considered the matter. "All right. But watch you don't disturb too much."

Wrapped up against the blustery winds, they retraced their steps of the night before, to the corner of the hotel, and across the rear car park, into the Old Inn.

Little had changed since the last time Joe saw the room. Rick's lighting equipment had been taken away for thorough examination, but the cupboard where Rick had hidden stood wide open, and so did the exit to the stables.

Joe stood in the centre of the room, Rick's cupboard behind him.

"All right," he said, "you're in your cupboard, Prudhoe enters. First question, how the hell could *he* see in the dark?"

"Torch," Rick said waving his hands in an imitation of someone using a flashlight. He pointed to the bottom of the

139

cupboard door which ended several millimetres from the floor. "Light from the room gets into the cupboard under the door and through my spy-hole."

Joe recalled he had seen light flickering in the Old Inn as he crossed the car park. "So what about the killer?" he asked.

Rick shrugged. "I only made the one light. When he ran, he took Prudhoe's torch with him."

"All the same, to attack him from behind in the dark means the killer had sussed the layout beforehand. As I've said all along, this was a planned killing." Joe brought his focus back to the room. "Right, so Prudhoe is dead. You come out of your cupboard. You hear me at the door and you run. Which way?"

Rick pointed to the stables exit. "Through there."

They moved from the old bar, into the stables.

Joe took in the scene of carnage that was the stack of disused furniture. He moved to the exit and looked out across the car park. From here, the whole rear of the hotel was in view, including the delivery entrance.

"At this point, you're thirty seconds behind the killer?" Joe asked. "You go to the door and look out to make sure the coast is clear. You didn't see him?"

Rick shook his head. "I didn't see no one. I saw the lights from the inn after you'd come in and switched them on. That was all."

Joe waved at the expanse of barren car park. "Your van was parked over there," he said pointing at the delivery point. "And from here, you ran to your vehicle and scarpered?"

Rick nodded.

"When I came round the corner of the hotel," Joe said, "you'd just stopped close to where Linda had come out. Then you suddenly drove off. Why?"

"You," Rick admitted. "I saw you in my wing mirror, figured I'd better, you know, shoot. I was gonna bell Linda this morning, but as you know, the plod nicked me in Selby."

Joe studied the rear of the hotel. There was one service entry, which he guessed led to the kitchens and the bar.

"What's the problem, Joe?" Cummins asked.

"Rick here was hyped up, in a hurry. He ran to his van, yet he saw no one else. So where was the killer? He – or she – was still in here." He gestured back at the stables. "Hiding amongst all that crap. He probably heard me bell the cops. And then I heard Rick's van start up, and I legged it, too. Five minutes later, I was on my way to my room for a shower, and the killer could have just ambled back into the hotel without trouble."

"The killer would have been soaking wet," Rick observed. "It was hammering down."

"That may let Geoff Vallance out," Joe speculated. "I met him in Reception and he was bone dry."

"What about Yvonne and members of Prudhoe's family?" Cummins asked.

"I can't vouch for them because I never saw them." Joe rolled another cigarette. "Terry, I think we need to speak to Deidre Prudhoe. She should have sobered up by now. Hannah, too, if she's calmed down." He turned on Rick. "You've been a damned idiot. If you hadn't run for it, we may well have had the killer last night."

Rick looked suitably rebuked. "I didn't know, did I?"

"Will you be charging him, Terry?"

"Certainly. Stealing by finding. Leaving the scene of a major crime." Cummins smiled evilly. "But I reckon you'll get off with a caution because by the time that girlfriend of yours is through with you, you'll be dog meat."

Rick gave them a hangdog pout.

Fishing out his disposable lighter, Joe said to Cummins, "One other thing."

"What?"

Joe held up the cheap lighter. "Where's my Zippo?"

***

141

They left Rick reunited with Linda, and Joe was reunited with his Zippo. Standing at the entrance, smoking, he broached the STAC's imminent departure with the Chief Inspector.

"I don't see why not, Joe," Cummins agreed. "You've been a great help and I don't think any of your crowd are implicated. What time is your coach due?"

"He's picking up at The Feathers, in Pocklington at ten o'clock. When I spoke to Keith, the driver, yesterday, he reckoned it would be going on eleven when he got here."

"That's no problem, Joe. If we can get to speak with a sober-ish Deidre Prudhoe and a calmer Hannah before then, you'll have done your civic duty."

Joe sucked on his cigarette. "You will let me know how it turns out, won't you? Only I write them up, you know."

"Of course, I know. Joe Murray's Casebook." Cummins laughed. "It'll be a lot easier for you these days, won't it? With computers and stuff."

Joe grinned. "A damn sight easier than that old Corona typewriter I used to use. And I print them through an internet POD publisher, you know. I even sell them as e-books."

"A bestselling author, too."

"Ha!" Joe's laughter was hollow and ironic. "I'm lucky to sell one a month." Taking a final drag on his thin roll-up, he stubbed it out. "Hadn't we better get on with it?"

Cummins agreed with a nod.

"I'll let Sheila and Brenda know that we can leave, and they can brief the rest of my party. Catch you up in Reception, Terry."

Passing through the narrow lobby, Joe paused at the counter where Yvonne was on duty. Asking after her movements the previous evening, her answer was scathing.

"I have no need to write anything down, Mr Murray. As I told you last night, I was in my room until Geoff called for me. After that, I was down here."

"You might think differently when Terry Cummins speaks to

you again," Joe retorted before carrying on into the bar and joining his two companions.

When he had done bringing them up to speed, Brenda sniggered. "Joe Murray beaten by a mystery he couldn't solve. Whatever next?"

"Time is what beat me, Brenda, not the problem," Joe pointed out. "We have under an hour before we pull out."

Brenda smacked her lips. "Life's not all about pulling out, Joe. Sometimes you have to put in. I tell you, one night with me…"

"I'll leave it to you two to tell the gang," Joe interrupted.

Sheila laughed and Brenda grinned.

Joe was about to rail them both when his mobile chirruped for attention. He checked the menu and read 'Cummins'. Puzzled, he made the connection. "Yeah? Terry?"

"Joe? Don't say anything. Just get up here. Room 209."

"Why? What's wrong?"

"Deidre Prudhoe. She's dead."

Chapter Thirteen

When he arrived on the second floor, Joe was escorted to the room by the same woman constable who had been in attendance for the previous night's interviews.

Joe felt only a few butterflies as Cummins let him into the room. He had seen the dead too many times for it to trouble him, but he still felt that tingle of nervousness, just as he had done the previous night when he had found Edgar Prudhoe.

Deidre Prudhoe lay flat on her back, arms straight down either side of her, open eyes staring up at the ceiling. A trickle of vomit had escaped her part open mouth and dribbled down her lip. Her right cheek had a bruise and scratch just above the jawbone.

"At first I thought she might have choked on her own vomit," Cummins said, "and she may well have done, but someone attacked her before she died." He pointed, following the line of the scratch and the bruise running down her jaw. "With her drunk and then slugged, it would be easy for someone to smother her with the pillow." He pointed to the item beneath Deidre's head.

Joe studied it, building up a picture in his mind of how it had happened. "First Edgar, now her. Why?"

"Well it's obvious, isn't it?" Cummins said. "She was in on the necklace fiddle – whatever was going on with the necklace – and so was a third party, as yet unknown, and that third party decided she should be silenced."

Joe shook his head. "That doesn't make a lot of sense to me, unless… have you spoken to Hannah and Callum yet?"

Cummins shook his head. "The daughter's out of it. So shocked she can hardly speak. And McGuire is with her. Says he's been with her all night."

"Terry –"

"Joe, I'm sorry, but you and your people won't be allowed to leave. I've called for our scientific support people, and I've asked the station to send down a full crew of uniformed men and women. I've got the deputy Chief Constable on his way, too, and he'll be breathing down my neck. I'll need a statement from everyone in the hotel before I can let you go."

Joe was about to argue, but thought better of it. Cummins, he knew, was right. "No problem. I'd better go back to the bar and let everyone know. And I'll have to ring our bus driver, tell him to hang about in Pocklington. You don't want him cluttering up the hotel along with your people. Terry, shocked or not, you'll have to get tough with Hannah Prudhoe. She's the only one who might be able to throw some light on this business."

Cummins nodded. "I'll get her downstairs and meet you there, but when the ACC arrives, you'll have to stand back."

Joe gave a grunting little laugh. "You leave Freddie Wainman to me."

Cummins was surprised. "You know the ACC?"

Joe nodded. "About two, maybe three years younger than me. I remember him when he was running round the streets of Sanford in short pants. Just the same as I remember you."

Relieved to be out of the room, Joe made his way hurriedly down to the bar, told Sheila and Brenda of the rearranged plans and rang Keith Lowry.

"I'm just getting 'em onto the bus," Keith complained.

"Then get 'em back off again. You come over here now and you'll find nowhere to park because the place is full of cops, and you'll still have a two-hour wait."

"You don't half know how to make my life hell, Joe Murray."

"Well, next time someone fancies doing a couple of murders, I'll ask 'em to wait until after we've gone." Fuming, he shut the phone down and found his two best friends looking curiously at him. "What?"

"A couple of murders?" Sheila asked.

Joe silently cursed himself for his lack of tact. Lowering his voice, he said, "Don't spread the word, yet, but Cummins has just found Deidre Prudhoe dead."

Brenda gawped. "Oh my God. How…"

Joe shushed her. "She was suffocated by the looks of it, but whoever did it tidied the room up after and tried to make it look as if she'd choked on her own vomit. Cummins will be here to announce it, soon."

"We'd better find a way of keeping the crowd entertained," Sheila said to Brenda.

"What about lunch, Joe?" Brenda asked.

"Wonderful. Here we are knee deep in bodies and all you can think of is food."

"Bog off," Brenda snapped. "I'm thinking of our members. You know what they're like."

"That's true," Sheila observed. "They say piranha fish can strip a horse to the bone in thirty seconds, but that's nothing at the side of the Sanford Third Age Club."

"I assume that the hotel will deal with it," Joe said, "but I don't know who's gonna foot the bill, and if they try stinging our lot for it, there could be a riot. I'll have a word with Yvonne Naylor."

Joe found Yvonne manning the counter, but her reception of him was distinctly cold, albeit helpful.

"Chief Inspector Cummins has apprised me of the situation, Mr Murray, and I've already spoken to Head Office. It's short notice, but we can arrange a cold buffet lunch and hot drinks. Accomplus will send the bill to the police, but alcoholic drinks will have to be paid for. I've also agreed to extend the room deadline. Normally, I would need your rooms cleared by ten.

Under the circumstances, I can extend that, but only by one hour. I have another party coming in this afternoon, and my staff will need time to prepare the rooms."

"Good of you, anyway," Joe said. "Wanna rethink your statement for Cummins?"

"I see no reason to," she shot back. "I told you where I was when Edgar Prudhoe was murdered."

"And what about later in the night? When Deidre was killed."

"I was in exactly the same place. Bed. My bed. Alone."

"So you can't prove it?"

Yvonne pulled in a deep breath and leaned as far over the counter as she could. In a whisper Joe could barely hear, she said, "It's a part of my job to be pleasant to people I can't abide, so I hope you'll forgive me when I tell you to bugger off and leave me alone."

Joe gave her a small round of applause. "At least that was honest, but it's the only thing you've said to me that I can be sure was the truth."

From Reception, Joe joined Cummins just as the Scientific Support team descended on room 209.

Brought into the meeting room, accompanied by her boyfriend, Hannah Prudhoe still looked pale and distant. When questioned by the Chief Inspector, she could throw no light on the murder of either of her parents.

"Your father was arrogant, bombastic and self-centred. The kind of man who must have enemies. Yet you're telling us, you knew nothing about them?"

Her anger began to bubble. "My father was a wonderful man, Mr Murray. He was kind, generous and doting. He couldn't do enough for me or my mother."

Joe almost commented on her mother's alcohol dependency, but bit his tongue just in time. She was, he realised, looking through a spoiled daughter's eyes.

"What about your mother, then?" he asked. "She came from

147

money, didn't she? Well-to-do-stock."

This time, Hannah's fury erupted. "The Hecklingtons, well-to-do? You should get your facts right. My grandfather, Sir Brian Hecklington, started out with nothing. He was an electrician, Mr Murray, and he built up his business from scratch, using nothing but his own skills, ingenuity, and sheer hard work. So no, they were not well-to-do. My father, too, built up his business interests and his political career from scratch. None of this has anything to do with marrying money or inheriting money."

A bell rang in Joe's head and he promptly backed off. "My apologies, young lady. I'm as eager as the next man to see these crimes solved, and I meant no offence. It just seemed to me to indicate something or someone in your family's past, and let's not forget, you could be next.

"Not while I'm here," Cal declared and Hannah squeezed his hand.

Ignoring the hubris and the young woman's simpering gaze, Joe stood up. "Terry, I'll leave you to question Hannah. I have something I need to check on."

Cummins appeared surprised. "Of course, Joe. And thanks for your help."

Joe came out of the room, only to find himself accosted by Sheila, Brenda, Les Tanner and George Robson.

"We have a mutiny on our hands, Joe," Brenda warned him.

"What the devil is going on, Murray?" Tanner demanded. "First we're told we're all right to pack and leave, and now we're told we can't leave because something else has happened, but we're not allowed to know what. If you had any idea of how to run the club, this sort of thing wouldn't happen."

"Tell me something, Les, do you naturally talk out of your backside or have you been army-trained? This has nothing to do with me. Terry Cummins told me we could leave. Ten minutes later, he told me we couldn't. Just calm down all of you and I'm sure it'll be sorted. The hotel is putting on a cold buffet for lunch so you won't starve to death."

"I have a date tonight, Joe," George complained. "I'd like to get back to Sanford in time to shower, shave and change."

"So what do you want me to do, George? Send a taxi and bring your date here. We're all in the same boat and there's nothing I can do about it."

"I tried to tell them, Joe," Sheila assured him.

"This," Tanner complained, "is like the fiasco in Filey when Eddie Roberts was killed."

"We can't plan for everything, Les," Sheila told him, "and the problem we had in Filey was at the police's behest, not Joe's."

"You tell 'em, Sheila," Joe approved. "What do you want us to do? Run an advert in the Sanford Gazette inviting all lunatics hell bent on murdering politicians and their families to steer clear of the hotels we book into?" he glowered at Tanner and George. "Now if you'll excuse me, I have some work to do. Why don't you go into the bar and watch the rugby on telly?"

"There is no rugby on telly," George shouted as Joe stepped into the lift. "It's football."

"Then watch the football," Joe called back as the doors closed.

Two minutes later, he was back in his room, unpacking his case, and pulling out his netbook. He had less than a quarter of an hour before officially vacating the room. He sat at the dresser, silently and impatiently urging the netbook to hurry up, but like a watched kettle, it refused to boil.

He stared out through the window on the Old Inn, the scene of Edgar Prudhoe's demise. Immediately beneath him, Rick and Linda were arguing with a pair of police officers. Joe guessed they probably had another gig to set up, perhaps in their home town of Bradford, and they would want to get home. He knew how they felt. He had to be back behind the counter of the Lazy Luncheonette in less than 24 hours, and he wanted to get home, too, get a little rest first.

The computer beeped to tell him it was ready. He opened the

internet browser, called up a search engine, typed in his query and as the results came through, he smiled broadly to himself.

He shut the machine down and packed it away again. Once this was done, he made a final check of the room to ensure he had left nothing behind, then grabbed the suitcase and came out.

What he had learned did not constitute proof, but Terry Cummins and his crew would find that. Joe had enough to accuse and maybe force a confession.

Stepping out of the lift on the ground floor, he left his suitcase with Sheila and Brenda in the bar, then strolled along the corridor to the conference room, where he found Cummins with Freddie Wainman, the Assistant Chief Constable.

"Long time no see, Joe," said Freddie, a tall, slender man with a distinguished shock of grey hair. The pair shook hands. "Terry has just been telling me of your efforts, and I'd like to thank you. However, as of now…"

"I know who did it and why," Joe cut him off.

The two officers exchanged a glance.

"Prematurely grey, Freddie," Joe said, and indicated his own, dark, curly mop. "You should learn to take a weekend off now and then. Try a ghost hunt at a hotel. Does wonders for your nerves."

"Knock it off, Joe," Cummins ordered. "This is the ACC you're talking to."

"Yes, and like I told you earlier, I remember Freddie when he was running round Sanford in short pants."

"And you were still in them, too, as I remember," said Freddie. "You say you know who did it and why. Are you going to enlighten us?"

"All in good time, Freddie. First we need…" He spotted a laptop on the table. "Whose is that?"

Cummins turned to see what Joe was talking about. "Oh, the computer? Edgar Prudhoe's. We thought it might throw a bit of light on matters, but if you've already cracked it, we won't need to bother."

"You think not? Terry, would you mind if I checked that machine over?"

Freddie laid a disapproving eye on Joe. "I thought you'd already solved it?"

Joe tucked himself in at the table and booted up the computer. "I have, but my evidence is a little thin. Maybe Edgar left more on here." He went into full persuasion mode. "Y'see, Freddie, if you've kept up to date with my activities, you'll know that like most amateurs, I don't have the same scientific back up as you boys. You're the ones who *prove* everything. I rely on my powers of observation and deduction to lead me to evidence and draw logical conclusions, which is what I've done this time. If the suspect argues, I could be in a difficult position, but if Edgar left something on there..." he let the idea hang.

Cummins and the ACC exchanged glances. Freddie nodded and Cummins said, "Help yourself, Joe. The ACC and I have to speak to the media." He gave a nervy laugh. "Downing Street breathing down our necks."

The two policemen left, and Joe powered up the machine. Its boot routine was slow, with three separate virus and spyware scans taking up the time, but once done, Joe looked on the desktop and shook his head at the dunderheadedness of Edgar Prudhoe. A man in public life had the right to protect himself against intrusion, but why didn't he lock the machine with a password?

He did not expect to find much, and he certainly did not expect to find anything other than a family link to Anglian, the electrical contract company started by his father-in-law. Prudhoe was too careful to leave any incriminating evidence lying around on an accessible computer, but if he did so in all innocence, then it might explain why the killer had waited so long.

The search proved fruitless. This machine had little to offer other than speeches to the Commons, and even they were only in rough draft form.

He was about to shut the machine down when the door burst open and Sheila burst in.

"Joe, unless you get out here and speak to the members, we are history."

"Tell them to knock it off or you'll set Brenda onto them," he ordered. "I've more on my plate right now, Sheila. I've almost cleared this business up and all I need is twenty minutes. After that, we should be allowed to get the bus here and go home. All right?"

"I'll try." Sheila disappeared again and Joe reached for the computer's power switch.

History, Sheila had said. Was it worth checking?

He opened up the internet browser, ignored the home page, which was the BBC political news, and instead, called up the browser history.

Here again, Edgar Prudhoe's lack of attention to detail left him wide open to cyber-attack. He was one of those men who never cleared out the history files, and when Joe looked deeper, he could see they stretched back for 100 days, taking him back to mid-July.

He scanned quickly through September and August and found nothing of any interest, but when he dropped into July, his blood ran cold. Search after search after search, and all for the same thing.

Joe felt his anger growing, but it was turned inward, aimed at himself. How could he have been so stupid?

He ran an internet search, learned what he wanted and after closing down the machine, he rushed out into Reception where he spotted Cummins talking with the ACC near the counter.

"Terry, do you have the pearls you found on Rick?"

Cummins nodded.

"Could I borrow them a moment?" Joe asked.

Cummins checked with Wainman who agreed, and Cummins then nodded to the policewoman who had sat in on the interviews and she hurried out of the hotel.

"What are you up to, Joe?" Cummins asked.

"I've just found something out and I want to test out my theory. If it pans out, I have your killer."

The constable returned with the pearls. Borrowing forensic gloves from her, Joe removed them from the evidence bag, took hold of the necklace at either end, and gently rubbed the two end pearls together.

"Smooth," he said. "As I expected."

Cummins frowned. "And?"

"Tell you in a bit. Right now, we need Hannah Prudhoe, Cal McGuire, Rick Hart, Linda Ellis, Yvonne Naylor and Geoff Vallance over at the Old Inn. I'll just talk to some of my people and I'll be with you."

"You're sure you know who it is?"

Joe smiled. "Five minutes, Terry."

Chapter Fourteen

When Joe arrived at the Old Inn, he found everyone sat around two tables which had been pushed together. Freddie Wainman and Cummins sat to the right hand end, the end towards the staircase. Next to them, nearer the stables exit, were Hannah and Callum McGuire. On the side nearest him as he entered were Yvonne, Geoff, Rick and Linda. Either side of the head of the table, closest the staircase, were Brenda and Sheila. Joe took the seat at the head where he could see everyone, plugged Edgar Prudhoe's laptop into a floor socket, and switched it on.

Waiting for it power up, he said, "This was one of the most puzzling cases I've ever dealt with. There were too many suspects, not one of whom could properly account for their movements at the time Edgar Prudhoe was killed and, of course, practically no one in the hotel could prove where they were when Deidre was murdered. Even those guests sharing rooms would be asleep. I had to look into quite a number of people before I finally arrived at the solution, but even without any research, I knew why Deidre was murdered. It was simply to shut her up because when she sobered up, she may have had information that would have pointed a finger straight at the killer."

Joe scanned the faces at the table. Most were impassive.

"Hannah, you're not going to like some of the things you hear, but it's better that you know about them now, before the press get hold of them, because they'll have a beano with it all." Joe addressed the whole group again. "Let's go back to the catalyst for this whole affair. The theft of the necklace. We know now that it was never stolen because it was never in the safe. Edgar wanted Callum McGuire out of his daughter's life. I don't think there's much wrong with Cal, but there you go. People, all people, take natural likes or dislike to others. Edgar did not like you, Cal, and he was prepared to try and buy you off. When he offered you ten grand to get the hell out, he wasn't about to give you money. He was about to offer you the pearl necklace he'd bought for his daughter. Its retail value was fifteen thousand, and he reckoned you'd get ten for it on the black market."

"That sounds about par for the course and the man," Cal agreed, and Hannah scowled at him as if he had betrayed her. "I'm sorry, Hann, but as Mr Murray's just said, your father hated me."

"Edgar's idea was simple," Joe went on. "He gave the necklace to Deidre so she could leave it in the Old Inn during the ghost walk. If and when you came to meet him after the walk, he would retrieve the necklace and offer it to you on condition that you disappear and never darken his daughter's knicker elastic again. But something happened that he couldn't count on. Linda earmarked Deidre as a dip on the ghost walk because Deidre was wearing the right kind of coat, one with deep pockets, and because Edgar Prudhoe had annoyed her, Linda, earlier. She was going to teach him a lesson. During the blackout, Rick ran round the crowd and dipped three pockets. Mine, Les Tanner's and Deidre's. He took my Zippo lighter, Tanner's Schaeffer pen, and a polythene bag from Deidre. The necklace was in that bag. When Deidre told Edgar, he came over to the Old Inn to get the necklace back, and while he was here, the killer, who had been waiting for him, took advantage of the situation. In a blind panic, Rick, who saw most of what happened, ran for it."

"We know most of this, Joe," Cummins said.

"You and I do, Terry, but these people don't," Joe gestured at the table in general. "It's important to recap because the events throw some light onto the killer. Rick told us he could only out make one flashlight in the Old Inn while he hid in the cupboard, and it belonged to Edgar Prudhoe. He was searching for the necklace. The killer, then, was working in total darkness alleviated only by the light of Prudhoe's torch, yet he – or she – managed to strike a single blow to the back of Prudhoe's head, which killed him. It means then, that we're dealing with someone who was either wearing a night vision lens – Rick – or someone who knows this building like the back of their hand – Linda, Yvonne, or Geoff."

Pandemonium broke out as the four he had accused shouted their innocence. When Cummins restored order, Joe went on.

"We cleared Rick. He didn't have time for the argument that would have preceded killing Edgar. We know it wasn't Linda. She was in the bar running the disco. That leaves us with Geoff and Yvonne. I ran a check on both their stories and both rang true, but one of them didn't tell us of a link to the Prudhoe family. It wasn't a link to Edgar, but to Deidre." Joe turned his head and stared. "Wasn't it, Yvonne?"

She held his gaze. "I don't know what you're talking about."

"I think you do," Joe retorted. "The fire at the Ferryman which took both your husband and your left hand. You never told us that the faulty wiring which caused the blaze had only been recently installed by a company called Anglian Electrical Contractors. I checked up on them, and the company founder was a man named Brian Hecklington. Hannah inadvertently put me onto it when she told me her granddad was a self-made millionaire who started out as an electrician just after the war. Brian Hecklington was Deidre's father, and as the Chairman of Anglian, in one sense, he could be viewed as the man who killed your husband. It was, after all, his cowboys who installed the faulty wiring."

Joe paused to see if Yvonne would react. Aside from spots of colour coming to her cheeks, she did not.

Joe pressed on. "Your plan, Yvonne, was not to take away

156

Edgar Prudhoe's life, but to take something from his wife, in the same way that the cowboys who worked for her father had taken from you."

The spots of colour rose. "Rubbish."

"If this is true, Joe," Cummins asked, "why was Deidre murdered?"

"Because she wasn't sober enough to give a toss about her husband's death," Joe replied. "Yvonne's retribution was a lesson Deidre would never learn. So our friendly hotel manageress decided that Deidre should pay the ultimate price, too."

Her face crimson with anger, Yvonne snapped, "This is complete nonsense. All right, yes I knew Sir Brian Hecklington was the founder of Anglian, and that Prudhoe was his son-in-law. I was mad as hell at his cowboys who did the job, and to this day I swear that the brewery colluded with Anglian to ensure the place caught fire. Billington's were desperate to get rid of that pub and the only way they could legally do it was to burn it down. I'm also willing to admit that seeing Prudhoe's reservation, persuaded me into asking for The Palmer. My hope was that I would find something, anything on him that I could use to discredit him." She faced Hannah. "I'm sorry, Ms Prudhoe, but your father and your grandfather were arrogant men, the kind I cannot abide, and the kind who, in my opinion, should never be allowed public office. I listened to my husband screaming while he burned to death thanks to your grandfather's insistence on cutting corners for greater profit." She swung back to Joe. "But I did not kill Edgar. I took my break yesterday evening, went to my room and stayed there until Geoff called me down."

"Can you prove that?" Cummins demanded.

Yvonne shook her head. "No. I can't."

"But it's probably true," Joe declared.

All eyes turned on him.

"What?" Cummins asked.

Yvonne was livid. "You have the temerity to accuse me, yet

you knew –"

Joe ignored the Chief Inspector and held Yvonne's gaze. "There should be a lesson in that for you," he interrupted. "Stop carrying the past around with you. I'm sorry you lost your husband like that, I'm sorry that Hannah has had to learn this way what cheapskates her grandfather's employees were. But you don't carry this kind of thing with you forever. I'm sure your husband was a fine man and he didn't deserve to die the way he did, but I'm equally sure Brian Hecklington had no intentions of killing Ronnie. It's done, however, and nothing will undo it. Like the wreckage of a broken marriage, the trick is to leave it behind and move on. You've carried that terrible night with you for the last fifteen years, and I can't imagine the pain you went through, emotional as well as physical, but you should move forward." He gestured at Geoff. "There's a fine young feller here who'd be ready to help you on that trail, if you dropped the wall and let him."

Geoff blushed. "Well, I, er…"

"And you should be more assertive, lad," Joe told him. "Forget her hand, and ask her for a date. The worst she can say is go to hell."

In the silence that fell, ACC Freddie Wainman spoke. "So we're in a situation where no one seems to have killed Prudhoe."

"Not quite," Joe corrected. "See, I kept linking this to the necklace, then I swung away from the necklace when I realised the remote connection between Yvonne and Deidre. A matter of a few minutes later, I learned that I had it right the first time. It was all about the necklace, and it's thanks to Brenda that I finally rumbled it."

"Me?" Brenda smiled modestly.

Joe nodded. "Brenda's a naughty woman. And she said something to me first thing this morning. 'Life isn't all about taking things out. It's also about putting things in.' Now we all know what Brenda meant by that and she's been ragging me all weekend, but it was then that it hit me. Stage magicians don't just take things, they place them, too. A man who can take a necklace from one pocket can also put it in another one, and that's exactly what Prudhoe wanted when he first approached you, isn't it, Rick?"

Rick's face coloured and Linda looked wary. "I, er, I dunno what you're talking about."

"Lies, lies, and more damned lies," Joe sighed. "All right, I'll spell it out. Edgar Prudhoe may have been a loudmouth and a bully, but he was no crook. The scenario I painted earlier, him willing to offer Cal the pearls, was crooked, and he would never do it. His reputation mattered too much to him. He would not arrange for the necklace to be stolen so he could claim on his insurance, because that is illegal. He could lose his seat for it, he could go to jail for it."

"Conspiracy to commit fraud," Cummins confirmed.

"If you say so, Terry," Joe conceded. "But Edgar did want rid of young Cal as we've already seen, so he needed someone who could safely plant the necklace on him. That way, Edgar would still get it back when Cal was exposed as a thief. Are you with me? Now who could safely plant the string of pearls? Edgar could try it himself, but it requires skills in sleight of hand and distraction, and if he was caught…" Joe let the idea percolate while he turned to Edgar's computer. "He needed a pickpocket, or better still, a stage magician."

With the machine running, Joe opened the internet browser, set it offline working, and called up the history.

"Edgar was a busy man. Businessman, politician, he didn't have time to fool around with trivia and, like so many other busy people, he never got around to deleting his browsing history. When I checked it, I found that he spent a lot of time in August looking for a conjuror. I also found a page from a Bradford newspaper which he'd downloaded. It detailed how a couple of local entertainers were found guilty of benefit fraud. Claiming dole while working the pubs and clubs of West Yorkshire. Rick and Linda." Turning the computer so that they could all see the page, Joe pointed at the couple. "Wanna tell us what happened next, or shall I go on?"

"So we got done for fiddling benefits," Linda grumbled. "We paid the money back and did our community service."

"I'm sure you did, but it also put Edgar Prudhoe onto you. I think I know what happened. Prudhoe approached you with a simple proposition. Rick, you steal the necklace from Deidre on the ghost walk. You'll be told in advance which pocket it's in. It was the simplest method of getting it out of Prudhoe's possession without implicating Prudhoe himself. Then, after the walk, you return to the bar where you slip it into Cal's pockets. The police turn up, everyone is searched, and there's Cal holding fifteen grand's worth of pearls which logically, he must have stolen from the safe at Prudhoe's home." Joe concentrated his stare on Rick. "How much did Prudhoe offer you?"

"I don't know what you're talking about," Rick insisted.

"Yes you do." When it became obvious that Rick would not rise to the challenge, Joe sighed. "All right, if you're not prepared to tell us, I'll carry on. You just stop me when I get it wrong. In between the day you agreed to do the job for Prudhoe, and last night, you came up with a plan of your own. I imagine Prudhoe offered you about five hundred to pull the stunt. I also imagine he showed you the necklace or more likely, gave you a photograph of it. That's the kind of man he was. Brash. A braggart. He'd want you to know that you were dealing with someone who mattered, someone who could afford to chuck away fifteen grand on trinkets. You had a better idea. With shiners worth fifteen thou' in your pocket you could be out of here and on the next ferry to Rotterdam. Prudhoe would be in a difficult position, wouldn't he? He'd colluded in this little scam and he could hardly go to the cops because you'd bubble him and shatter his precious reputation. Having said that, there was still a danger that he might set a few private eyes on you, so somewhere along the line, you decided that the only safe solution was to get rid of him altogether. You took the pearls as you were supposed to, and then, when you didn't turn up in the bar, he decided to come over to the Old Inn, where you were waiting for him. You killed him and then ran for it."

"Hang on, Joe," Freddie Wainman cut in. "You said earlier, that Rick didn't have time to kill Prudhoe."

"No. I said he didn't have time to argue with Prudhoe before killing him. The truth is, he never had any intentions of arguing with Prudhoe. He was intent purely on killing him."

"If that's so, the best thing for him to do, then, would be to leave The Palmer altogether," Cummins said.

"And point the finger straight at himself?" Joe argued. "You couldn't do that when you just committed cold-blooded murder, could you Rick? Not with everyone else but you and me still in the hotel. We'd be the only suspects."

All eyes concentrated on the entertainer. He stared wildly about the room, then kicked back his chair and ran for it. Before anyone could react, he yanked open the door, only to find George Robson blocking his way. Rick turned and rushed for the stables exit, shrugging off Geoff's outstretched arms. He pulled the door open and found both Alec Staines and Les Tanner in his way.

"Sit down, Rick," Joe ordered. "You're not going anywhere without a police escort, and we're not through yet."

With Rick marched back to his seat and Alec, George and Les guarding the exits, Joe dropped back into his narrative.

"Prudhoe was actually the major architect in his own death. He was going to frame Cal for stealing the necklace, so Rick decided to frame Cal for the murder too, and it wasn't difficult. He stole Cal's jack handle. Simple enough to do. Cal was in the hotel most of the evening while Rick was here, in the Old Inn. Using the Land Rover's jack handle would hang both the theft and killing firmly on Cal's shoulders." Joe waved vaguely at Rick. "In order to do so, he'd need to plant evidence on Cal."

Joe broke off from his narrative and concentrated on Chief Inspector Cummins. "Terry, if you check the necklace you found on Rick, you'll find it's a fake. That's what I was doing when I asked for it a little while ago. When I realised what was going on, I went online to learn how I could tell the real thing from fakes. If you rub two pearls together and they feel sandy or gritty, then they're real. If they feel smooth, they're almost certainly fake. You need your boys to verify it, but for my money, that necklace is a fake. I'm willing to bet that he and Linda paid no more than fifty pounds for it. The idea was simple. Rick would pass the fake necklace to Linda, and she could plant it on Cal. Over the years they've been together, Rick has obviously taught Linda some of his conjuring tricks. She knew how to get the necklace into Cal's pocket. You and your people turn up, Terry, everyone is searched and Cal is now caught with the shiners and it's his jack handle that killed Prudhoe. Cal is looking at life, while these two get away with and pocket the real shiners to boot."

"I can see gaping hole in this," Cummins announced. "If this is what Rick and Linda planned, the sensible thing to do would be to leave the pearls with Linda throughout the evening."

Joe smiled. "With Prudhoe screaming for the police to be brought in and everyone to be searched? Not likely. Prudhoe had everything well organised. The birthday announcement would take place before the ghost walk. The police had to get here from York, which would take at least an hour, and in the meantime, pressure from the guests would ensure that the ghost walk went ahead, so Rick could carry out the original theft and have time to plant the pearls on Cal."

"So all Edgar Prudhoe's ranting in my office was just that?" Yvonne asked. "Hot air."

"Yes and no," Joe agreed. "Edgar definitely needed the cops here, but not too early. There were a lot of variables. Suppose you called out a local constable? Suppose there was a patrol car in the area? Edgar could have worked his way round those problems by demanding that a senior detective was called to investigate properly, and obviously, while we waited, he would graciously consent to the ghost walk going ahead. In the end, it didn't matter to him, because I persuaded him to let me investigate, and that played into his hands. But for Rick and Linda…" Joe toyed with the computer keyboard while glancing around his audience. "They could not afford to have the fake necklace in Linda's possession until after Prudhoe was dead."

"You're a fantasist," Linda snapped. "I deny it. All of it."

"A fantasist, am I? What were you doing outside the hotel when I came round the corner?"

Her cheeks coloured. "I, er, Rick rang me. He wasn't making sense. I came to see what was going on."

"He rang you?" Joe asked. "When he rang you earlier, you couldn't hear him."

The blush deepened. "I mean he texted me."

Joe shook his head. "He didn't have time to put a text together, unless it was a pre-planned one, and he couldn't have done that because he had no way of knowing in advance that I would be there." Again he took in everyone around the table. "You see, that's what went wrong for them. The one thing they couldn't plan on. Someone, me, following Edgar Prudhoe to the Old Inn. When Rick realised I was right behind Edgar, he had to think on his feet, and when people are forced to react, they make mistakes. He could have waited, and attacked me. But that would be risky. He took Edgar by surprise and in the dark. Anyone else coming in would probably switch on the lights, and anyway, he didn't actually know it would be me. It could have been Geoff, George Robson, even a cop. So he ran for it, trying to stick to his original plan, but as he stopped alongside Linda, I came round the corner. He saw me in his mirror and drove off. Linda was screaming after him. I thought she was screaming for him to come back, but she wasn't. She was screaming because he hadn't given her the fake pearls to plant on Cal."

"Total garbage," Linda declared. "Every word of it."

"We'll decide on that, young lady," Wainman said. "Go on, Joe."

Joe grunted his thanks. "Rick's thinking wasn't totally out of the loop. He's an entertainer, a conjuror, and a lot of their work involves thinking quickly and distracting the audience's attention. When he saw me come round the corner, he knew he couldn't hand the pearls to Linda, because I would have seen him do it. So he scrammed and turned left out of the hotel, as if he was heading for York. That was clever. Everyone would assume he was making for his home in Bradford, and he could double back, down the road to Selby and then onto Hull. He was carrying the fake pearls, but he had time to work on that while he was driving away. He realised that if he was caught, he could admit to trying to steal the necklace. He knew that you would be so busy with Edgar's murder that he'd probably get off with a fine or even a caution. Especially when the pearls turned out to be fake, which is something we'd all have blamed Edgar Prudhoe for, and if you remember, Terry, when we questioned him, he eventually admitted he'd been trying to get away with the necklace."

"I remember," Cummins said with a frown. "Surely, Joe, if he'd managed to plant the necklace on young McGuire, someone would have recognised it as a fake."

"Hannah wouldn't," Joe said, "and neither would Cal, because neither of them had seen the originals." Joe paused to add emphasis to his next words. "But Deidre might have."

Light dawned in Cummins' eyes. "And that's why she was murdered?"

"I think so," Joe agreed with a solemn nod. "At least, I'm sure it was part of their thinking. If everything had gone according to plan, Deidre wouldn't have been a problem. She was a drunk. How accurate was her memory? Would she realise the switch? It became an academic question anyway, because they weren't able to plant the fake necklace on Cal, as a result of which Cal was never accused, which meant that Deidre then became a threat. They didn't know how much she might have known about Edgar's little plan, and we were all looking for someone other than Cal, so Deidre had to be silenced."

"Not by Rick," Wainman argued. "He was in custody overnight."

"Correct," Joe agreed. "It was Linda."

"You're lying," she cried. "How could I get into her room? Ask Geoff, ask Yvonne. Did I ask for a pass key?"

"You didn't need one," Joe replied. "When Linda came in out of the rain with me last night, Geoff loaned her a set of hotel clothes until hers dried. My guess is, she waited until the early hours, then came out of her room dressed in those hotel clothes, knocked on Deidre's door, and Deidre, still half drunk, let her in, thinking she had come to attend to something in the room. Instead, Linda knocked her cold and smothered her with the pillow. That's where the bruise and scratch came from on Deidre's chin."

"I deny it," Linda repeated, louder this time.

Joe dug into his pocket and threw a ballpoint to her. "Do me a favour, Linda. Take a piece of paper and write out, 'Joe Murray is a liar'."

"So you can compare my handwriting? Not likely."

"Do it in capitals," Joe suggest while Cummins pushed a notebook at her.

Her eyes filled with suspicion, Linda opened the notebook and picked up the pen.

With it poised over the paper, Joe shouted, "Stop." He looked around the table. "Did you all notice that?"

Everyone appeared puzzled.

"Notice what?" Sheila asked.

"Linda is left handed."

The assembled faces were still puzzled.

"What about it?" Cummins asked.

"The bruise and scratch were on Deidre's *right* cheek. Whoever hit her is left-handed." Joe pointed at her engagement ring. "And it doesn't matter how much you may have cleaned and polished your ring, Linda, the police scientists will still find traces of Deidre on it."

Linda remained tight lipped and silent.

"So the only question we need answering is, where are the real pearls?" Cummins asked.

"Do you wanna tell us what you did with them, Rick?" Joe asked. "Or shall I make another educated guess?"

Rick, too, remained silent.

"All right, here we go again." Joe heaved a sigh. "If Rick was going to be caught, it had to be while he was carrying nothing or carrying the fakes. So he hid the real ones in this building," Joe gestured around him. "He knew you'd have people working here, but once you were through and you had Cal arrested, he or Linda could come back and retrieve them. It didn't matter how long they had to wait. Hours, days, even a couple of weeks."

The Chief Inspector shook his head. "My people searched this place last night. If those pearls were here, they'd have turned up."

"True." Joe pointed to the door where Alec Staines and Les Tanner stood sentry. "But did they search all that crap in the stables? No they didn't, because nothing happened in the stables, did it? Rick knew he couldn't leave them in here precisely because your boys would have found them, so as he made his escape through the stables, while I was in here looking at Prudhoe's body, he hid them somewhere in there. Get your people to turn the place inside out and they'll find them."

Rick and Linda glowered. "You can't prove one word of this," Linda challenged.

"No I can't," Joe agreed, "but I don't need to. The police will do that now that Terry knows where to look." Joe smiled. "So you'd better start thinking about how you'll explain it all."

***

Joe signed off the Sanford Third Age Club receipts and

166

tucked his copy into his wallet. "No peace for the wicked. I have to spend this afternoon bringing the club accounts up to date, now," he grumbled.

Putting the hotel's copy to one side, Yvonne smiled. "You're a remarkable man, Mr Murray. Did you know that?"

"I keep trying to tell others, but they won't listen."

Now Yvonne laughed. "You're the unlikeliest detective I've ever come across. Not that I've met many, but you still stand out."

Behind her, Geoff emerged from the office and cast a fond smile in her direction before leaving Reception for the bar.

"And you're not bad at matchmaking," Yvonne whispered.

Joe glanced from her to Geoff's departing back and then at Yvonne again. "You two are an item?"

Yvonne found the notion humorous. "There's a long way to go before we can say that, but Geoff has asked me out to dinner later in the week. Too early to see where it may lead, but I've agreed and I'll have to see if I can forget about this." She held up her deformed hand.

Joe gave her a wrinkled grin. "Sanford is a mining town, you know. The pits are long gone, but when I was growing up, I saw many a man missing hands, arms, legs. We had our share of war wounded too. Some of them got depressed about it, and their lives were never the same again. But others… It was like nothing had happened to them. They adjusted. I don't know what you went through on that night, and God forbid that I should ever have to learn. I feel for you. But it's up to you whether you carry it around for the rest of your life, or put it behind you and start afresh. Good luck to you both."

He turned from Reception and bumped into a still-distressed Hannah holding Cal's hand.

"We just wanted to say thank you, Mr Murray," Hannah said.

"I'll send you a bill." Joe winked to show he was only joking. "I'm sorry, young lady. Sorry for your loss, but I hope you two will come to terms with it and make the best of your lives."

"You helped bring those two to justice, and for that we're grateful," Cal pointed out. "As for Hann and me... we have a long time ahead of us." He offered his hand and Joe shook it. "Thanks again."

***

With the clock approaching two in the afternoon, Keith slowed down to come off the motorway for the final mile into Sanford. As he did so, Joe said, "See you," and closed up his mobile phone.

Sheila and Brenda raised expectant eyebrows at him.

"Terry Cummins," he said. "They went through the stables and found the real pearls hidden in an old bedside cabinet amongst all the junk, just as I said they would. The minute he confronted Rick and Linda with them, they both started to talk. Linda admitted killing Deidre and Rick has confessed to killing Edgar. Linda's ring has been taken away for analysis, and Rick's clothing has, too. Terry figures that when Rick hit Edgar, enough skin, hair and blood will have flown up into the air for some of it to land on Rick's clothing. They're both blaming each other for coming up with the scheme."

Sheila tutted. "They're not much more than children, either of them."

"Well, they're going to grow up a lot behind bars," Brenda commented. "What do you think, Joe? Twenty-five years each?"

"Cold-blooded murder," he said, "and it was for financial gain. Fifty years ago, they'd have hung for that... well, Rick would. For my money, they still should, the pair of 'em."

"You mean hanged, not hung," Sheila clucked again. "And there's no evidence to support the idea that hanging is a deterrent, Joe."

"You've been reading *The Guardian* again," Joe protested. "And anyway, who said anything about a deterrent? It's a

168

punishment. Remember when we were at school, if we did something wrong, we got six of the best. It taught us that misbehaviour hurts."

"It also taught us that the people in charge get it wrong now and again, too," Brenda pointed out. "Like the time you got a whacking for fighting in the schoolyard, and it wasn't you. Remember?"

"I remember. It was you."

The two women laughed.

"That's the trouble with the death penalty, Joe," Sheila said. "When they get it wrong, how do you put it right?"

Joe shrugged. "Maybe you should visit a séance and ask Edgar and Deidre Prudhoe how they feel about it."

Heaving a sigh, Sheila said, "Well, that's another thrilling weekend outing for the Sanford Third Age Club. Christmas is the next one. I wonder what might go wrong then."

Brenda gazed up as if seeking divine inspiration. "The only thing I can think that may go wrong is Joe."

He frowned. "Me?"

"You may have to spend some money."

THE END

Fantastic Books
Great Authors

Meet our authors and discover our exciting range:

- Gripping Thrillers
- Cosy Mysteries
- Romantic Chick-Lit
- Fascinating Historicals
- Exciting Fantasy
- Young Adult and Children's Adventures

Visit us at:
www.crookedcatpublishing.com
Join us on facebook:
www.facebook.com/crookedcatpublishing

Printed in Great Britain
by Amazon